When  Greek village of Simitra, it destroys the home of the Patagos family and orphans twelve-year-old Porphyras and his little sister, Mina. Desolate, but united in their deep affection for each other, they vow that no matter what happens to them, or where they're sent, they will never allow themselves to be separated.

Offered a new home by a kindly family in far-off Holland, Porphyras is overjoyed, but Mina finds herself unable to adjust to the cold, wet climate and the alien ways of the people in the Dutch village. Porphyras does everything he can to cheer her, but she continues to long for the bright sun and brilliant sky of their native Greece. One especially gloomy day, she goes for a lonely walk along the seashore—and vanishes, leaving no trace.

Nearly mad with worry and grief, Porphyras rejects the idea that his beloved sister may be dead, and clings to the belief that he will have word from her, that they will be reunited again. Following up the slimmest of clues, he runs away from the Dutch village and sets out across Europe in a desperate search—a search that takes years, and involves him in adventures and disappointments which test every bit of his determination, ingenuity and faith.

A CRITERION BOOK
FOR YOUNG PEOPLE

THE ORPHANS OF SIMITRA

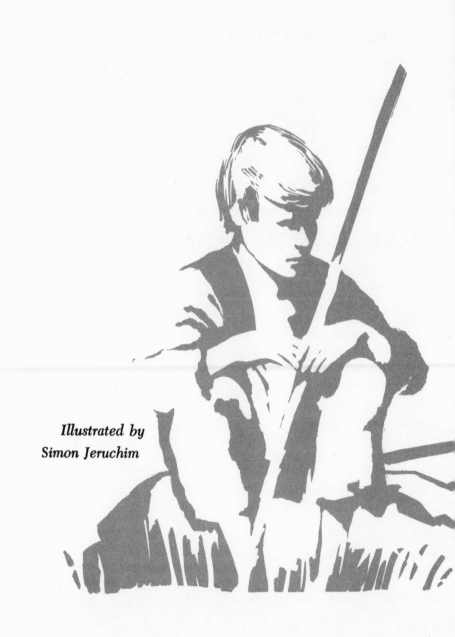

Illustrated by
Simon Jeruchim

The
Orphans
of
Simitra

PAUL-JACQUES BONZON

Translated from the French
by Thelma Niklaus

Criterion Books   New York

jB644lor

First American edition 1962

Library of Congress Catalog Card Number: 62-8944

English translation © 1957
by the University of London Press Ltd

First published in France in 1955
by Librairie Hachette
under the title Les Orphelins de Simitra

Designed by The Etheredges

Manufactured in the United States of America

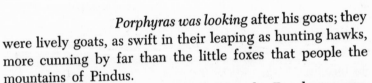

1

Porphyras was looking after his goats; they were lively goats, as swift in their leaping as hunting hawks, more cunning by far than the little foxes that people the mountains of Pindus.

Looking after the goats never brought Porphyras anything but trouble. All the same, he liked to go along with them to the hills. For then the whole sky was his; and the sky over Greece is very beautiful.

While his charges roamed where they pleased, horns held high and beards lifted by the wind, Porphyras would stretch out full length on the sun-scorched turf and look up at the sky, staring at it unwaveringly.

On this particular day, Porphyras was turning over in his mind a wonderful idea. He was staring at the road, the high-road that climbed the mountain slopes from Konitza to amble through olive groves until it reached the beautiful bay of Arta, set in the rock like a lake.

Even though all Greeks, whether grown-up or only twelve, like Porphyras, have the germ of poetry within them, they

7

never forget that their land is poor. They have to live: they can go barefoot for most of the year, make do with a bowl of goat's milk and a handful of olives when they are hungry, shelter from the cold in a rough cabin: but they must at least possess a roof, goats, and olive trees.

Porphyras' father did in fact possess these things, but the cabin was tumbledown; there were only three goats, and those nearly dry; and a few olive trees so old that they no longer had the strength to bear fruit. Hardly a week went by without his father saying:

"The children are growing so fast—we won't be able to feed them."

"What can we do?" sighed his mother.

"I don't know . . . perhaps leave here and look for work in the marble quarries . . ."

And his mother began to weep again, for she could not imagine leaving, just like that, the poverty-stricken countryside that had given them birth.

One day the father had a brainwave.

"Suppose we take over that old shanty by the roadside; no one uses it for anything."

"What would we do with it?"

"Turn it into a garage."

The mother laughed.

"A garage? . . . We haven't even got a car—and with our miserable little savings we're not likely . . ."

"A garage for repairing the cars that go by. There's only one mechanic in Simitra, and none at all along the road."

"My poor Christophore, you don't know the first thing about cars—you've only driven bullock carts and wheelbarrows!"

"I can learn. And Constantine and Porphyras can help me."

"And the tools you need—where will they come from?"

"I'll buy some."

"What will you use for money?"

8

"I'll borrow some."

And that is why, for two years now, tourists traveling along the sun-baked road that winds between Konitza and Arta have been able to read these words on a dilapidated hut by the wayside—THE PATAGOS SERVICE STATION. Underneath, the unaccustomed hand of Christophore Patagos had added: *Repairs—Breakdown Service.* The word GASOLINE was unfortunately missing.

That was Porphyras' wonderful idea, his great dream— to have a gasoline pump. That is what he was thinking about that day as he looked after his goats. This idea had been with him a long time, in fact ever since his father took him to the fair at Janina. Janina is not a big town; but since it is set at the junction of two main roads, it carries considerable traffic. On the outskirts of the town a modern service station had been built, all white, with gold lettering, and a magnificent gasoline pump standing sentinel at each side of the door. Porphyras had stood gasping with admiration in front of the person who was working them: a boy not much taller than himself, dressed from head to foot in scarlet overalls, and wearing a cap as loaded with gold as the shopfront itself. There he stood in front of the garage, straight as a cypress, waiting for customers. Every time a car stopped, the little scarlet gnome rushed forward, brought up a long tube, unscrewed the cap, solemnly pressed a button and filled the tank. Then, as the car, filled now to the brim, set off in clouds of blue smoke, he bowed politely, one hand to the peak of his gold-braided cap. For two whole hours Porphyras stood there, as motionless as the gasoline pumps: he would have been there still if his father, bathed in perspiration, crimson with fury, and dragging his newly-acquired nanny goat on a rope, had not snatched him from his contemplation.

From that day Porphyras had only one ambition: to wear red overalls and be in charge of a gasoline pump.

Sitting on the slope, he looked along the road: cars passed

and overtook each other. They were of all kinds, from the
decrepit and outdated cars of the small shopkeepers of the
area to the beautiful chromium-plated models loaded with
luggage that whizzed by silently and speedily, raising clouds
of dust behind them. These were the ones that interested
him most.

What far-distant country had they come from? Where
were they going? Before his eyes danced the image of the

little red gnome at Janina. Oh, when would his father set up a gasoline pump?

It must be confessed that very few cars stopped at the shabby Garage Patagos, where the only tools were a jack that didn't work properly, and about half a dozen wrenches. The only tourists that pulled up in front of its doors were those who had no choice. Papa Christophore found himself called upon mainly to mend inner tubes. It would cost a great deal to set up a gasoline pump. A big storage tank would have to be excavated underground, and where would they find the money?

Propping his head on his hand, and once again letting his goats crop the maize, Porphyras said to himself: "If only more tires got punctures, say four or five a day at ten *drachmas* a time, it would make quite a good amount by the end of a month. Papa Christophore would have enough money to set up a pump."

He thought, "After all, it isn't really impossible: the road has many rough spots in it; the day before yesterday two cars had to stop."

He was deep in all sorts of calculations when he heard the distant sound of a powerful engine. A heavy truck loaded with gravel was bumping over the uneven surface of the road. Feeling vaguely uneasy and filled with foreboding, he watched it approach. The big truck went by, continued on its way, then turned in toward the lower side of the road and drew up between two cedars. He rose to his feet, staring with all his eyes, and saw the tip rising toward the sky, so that the gravel slid down with the rushing sound of a waterfall. Porphyras turned pale. They were going to repair the road, to tar it. No more punctures, no gasoline pump, no boy in red with a gold-braided cap. He rubbed his eyes on his cuff, and ran off.

2

Porphyras had a sister, whose name was Marina, though everyone at home called her Mina. She was ten years old, with sparkling eyes in a face the color of a ripening olive, and hair blacker than the leaves of cypresses outlined against the sky. Porphyras was very fond of her, without knowing exactly why. Maybe it was because he felt it his duty to look after her, since he was two years older than she was; or maybe because Mina was very sweet and very pretty. There had never been a quarrel between them, nor a secret. Porphyras used to tell his sister all the silly things he did—and they were many—knowing that she would never give him away.

So when he brought the goats back, Porphyras went straight to his sister. The little girl realized immediately that her brother had something important on his mind by the way he was fumbling with the end of his belt.

"Mina—you know my red overalls . . . ?"

"Yes?"

"I won't ever have them, nor the cap with the gold braid

13

. . . They're going to mend the road, I'm sure of it. They've already brought the gravel, and they're going to put tar down. I've seen the barrels."

He had not in fact seen any barrels; only his lively imagination made him feel that he had. Mina tried to comfort him by saying that, even so, Papa Christophore would still have work to do. All to no purpose, however, for Porphyras could not be convinced.

Mina had always had tremendous admiration for her brother; first because he was a boy, then because he was bigger and stronger than she was, and lastly because he was always ready to climb trees to get pomegranates or figs for her. Once, when he had gone rushing off into the mountains, he had even brought back a tiny newborn jackal for her, and she had looked after it until the day it escaped from its cage. But her admiration, already so great, reached its peak the day Porphyras told her about the wonderful red uniform. She immediately saw her brother in his glowing scarlet overalls, standing in front of the handsome Patagos Service Station, supplying gallons of gasoline. Even the ancient god Zeus sitting on his throne in Olympus would cut a very poor figure beside Porphyras.

So now Mina was as miserable as her brother, and her disappointment was as keen as his. Two days passed, and all the time Porphyras went around frowning and looking worried. Then he said to his sister:

"Mina, I've got an idea!"

"I knew it."

"How?"

"I just knew you'd have one in the end; you always do."

"Have you still got some money in your money box?"

"Not very much, Porphyras."

"How much?"

"About twenty *leptas*, that's all."

"That'll be enough."

"What are you going to buy?"

14

"Promise not to tell?"

"Of course."

"Then place your little finger against mine and we'll blow."

Mina raised the little finger of her right hand, Porphyras did the same, and they blew on them. That is how children in Epirus pledge themselves to keep a secret.

Then Porphyras leaned toward his sister and whispered in her ear a long and rambling explanation.

"Oh!" And Mina's mouth grew round. "That's what you're going to do?"

"There's no harm in it, is there?"

"I don't know—I think there is."

"Don't you want to see me in red overalls and gold braid?"

"Of course I want you to have your red outfit, but . . ."

"What would you do, then, in my place?"

The little girl hesitated; she found it difficult to reply. She had no wish to hurt her brother, and yet . . . She simply smiled gently at him, lifting her beautiful dark eyes to his face. That was all the encouragement Porphyras needed.

"You'll see, Mina! I'll have my red overalls before Pindus is white with snow! Will you go and fetch your twenty *leptas*?"

The little girl went to rummage in the cupboard where she kept her things, took out her money box, a little cardboard box that had once contained pepper, and counted out twelve, fifteen, nineteen *leptas*.

"Look, Porphyras, my box is empty now."

"It'll soon be full again. Soon we'll be rich, and you won't go barefoot any more. And you'll have a lovely dress with birds embroidered on it!"

Every evening Porphyras went to the village with the surplus goats' milk. The grocer's shop was a sort of general store, where a little of everything was sold: brooms, long-stemmed Greek pipes, fly swatters, and nails as well. He

15

went up to the drawers containing nails. There were some of every size, but he was mainly interested in the smallest, blue gleaming nails with wide flat heads.

"I'll have nineteen *leptas'* worth," he said, putting his money on the counter.

The grocer's wife placed a sheet of paper on the scales, and Porphyras watched her pouring one, two, three handfuls of tacks onto it.

"As many as that?" he said, almost scared by the quantity.

His empty can in one hand, his paper full of nails in the other, he left the village behind. It was dusk: the sun had just disappeared over the horizon into the invisible sea that stretched, as Porphyras well knew, at the foot of the white hills. He lifted his eyes to the sky, where the first stars were just beginning to appear, then looked down at his paper bag.

"Stars," he thought, "are a bit like nails fixed in the sky."

He smiled at the comparison he had just made, and then it disturbed him. The stars were beautiful golden nails that delighted the eyes of men, while his nails, what use would they be?

He was on the point of throwing them away, when the sound of a car humming along the highroad reached him.

"Stars are stars and nails are nails," he said, quickly putting things straight in his mind.

He came to the highroad. Night was falling. He sat down by the roadside and opened the paper carefully to count his nails. He soon gave up; there were too many. Then he bent down, and put a tack, pointed end up, on the road. It balanced perfectly—these were just the nails he needed. He was filled with rapture. His head whirled with figures, calculations, additions. Four hundred nails: four hundred punctures. It was fabulous. What a lot of *drachmas* in Papa Christophore's pockets. Before ever the first soft flakes of snow fell upon Pindus, the gasoline pump would be set up in front of the handsome Patagos Service Station; he him-

16

self would put on his red overalls for the first time. . . . Mina would have her dress with birds on it, Mother the set of kitchen utensils she had coveted so long, big brother Constantine his gun; and Papa Christophore could smoke Thracian cigars all day long.

Gradually night settled down upon the countryside, almost as dark as the yews on the hillside. Porphyras, putting down his milk can, walked to the middle of the road, crouched on his heels, and with infinite care began to put his nails, point upright, here and there upon the surface, saying as he placed each nail, "Ten *drachmas*—ten more *drachmas*." He had put down more than fifty; that was plenty; though he would have scattered more if an oxen cart, returning late to a farm, had not come along and interrupted him.

He ran off home, where his mother was just beginning to grow anxious.

Porphyras' home was a very simple one: there was a big kitchen on the ground floor and above it a loft, in one half of which the three children slept. It was very hot in the loft in summer, so the children preferred to sleep out of doors, under the big fig tree that sheltered them like a roof. They would unroll their straw mattresses at the foot of the tree and sleep soundly all night long.

That evening Mina pulled her mattress still closer to her brother's: and as soon as they were lying down she asked in a whisper:

"Did you put them down?"

"Not all—still, Papa Christophore will have plenty of work tomorrow."

Mina sighed.

"Won't he be surprised?"

"Oh, he'll only think the road's getting worse and worse."

Mina made no reply. But Porphyras, beneath the fig tree that sheltered them like the outspread wing of a mighty eagle, stayed with his eyes wide open, instead of closing them in sleep, his ears strained to catch every sound from the bottom of the hill, where the highroad ran by.

And he went on counting . . . fifty nails, fifty punctures; a hundred nails, a hundred punctures. But the more he counted and the bigger the figures became, the less happy he felt. Why was it that Mina could not share his own excitement? Why, just before she fell asleep, had she sighed like that, as if she were sad? He turned toward his sister, and covered her small hand, holding a branch of wild lavender like a bouquet, with his own. But he dared not wake her up. What could he say?

Suddenly, the calm of that warm night, shrouding the Greek countryside like a velvet curtain, was pierced by a beam of light, and almost at once there was the sound of a distant car approaching. He shivered. He was assailed by all sorts of ideas that had never occurred to him before. That car approaching—did it belong to some poor local shopkeeper, returning late with his wares—or was it the doctor's car from Simitra, setting out to visit a patient?

He listened intently, trying to make out the type of car by the sound of its engine, which he was quite good at doing. It was a steep slope, and old cars rattled as they climbed it. No, the one approaching was not an old boneshaker; it was swallowing up the cedar-lined slope far too easily. It was a big touring car in a hurry. He was filled with sudden joy again; but it was gone in a flash. Suppose children were sleeping in that unknown car, a little girl like Mina resting at ease on its cushions . . . the car had nearly reached the nails . . . it was among them . . . a sharp, wicked point stuck into the tire and ripped it, the tire went flat, the car was traveling so fast it skidded and crashed into an enormous cedar. . . .

Porphyras sat bolt upright on his pallet, his heart thudding and his forehead damp with sweat. With his nerves stretched to breaking point, he listened. The car had reached the top of the slope; its headlights no longer swept

18

the sky. It went past the fig tree like a whirlwind and, devouring the night with its great yellow eyes, it disappeared. Porphyras drew breath again, very much relieved: but he was too shaken to calm down. Other cars would go by, and every time he would endure the same horror. He rose to his feet. It was a moonless night, but the stars of Greece shine with such splendor that the nights are never entirely dark. He walked along the deserted road, and came to the summit of the steep cedar-lined slope at the foot of which slumbered Simitra. He recognized the big tree where he had stopped on his way back from taking the milk. This was the place. How could he find the nails again?

He knelt down on the roadway, stretched out his hand and felt carefully over the stones. He found only one small overturned nail.

"They're not dangerous on their sides like that," he murmured. "Let's look for the others first."

He began to pat the surface of the road with the flat of his hand, until a sharp point dug into his palm. He put the nail in his pocket, and thought sadly of the beautiful uniform he would not be getting after all.

A few inches along, another nail pricked his hand, and farther on, another.

Then, one after the other, he picked up four nails.

He was still at it, trying to pick up tacks until none was left, when a sweeping headlight announced the approach of a car. It was a long way off: he would have plenty of time to move out of the way. On all fours, he went on combing the surface of the road. Here was another nail, perhaps the very one that might have thrown the car against the big cedar. There were still plenty more. In his frenzy, he took no more notice of the lights that showed now left, now right, according to the winding of the road. Here was another nail . . . another . . .

Suddenly the car was there, at the bend. The road was flooded with a spray of light. Porphyras turned his head,

19

and his eyes were dazzled with the sudden glare of the headlights. In that awful moment he could not remember which side of the road was nearer. The lights mesmerized him: he thought it was coming straight at him. Instead of throwing himself on the grass at the side, he ran right across the whole width of the road.

There was a screeching of brakes; a bump; then terrified cries coming from the car. Porphyras felt himself spinning around several times; his arms flailed out in a desperate attempt to regain his balance; then he fell, rolled over onto a pile of stones, and was still.

After a terrifying skid, the car came to a halt a few yards ahead. Its occupants flung themselves out and shone a flashlight along the road.

"Merciful heavens!" said a woman's voice. "We've killed a child!"

Even as hands were stretched out to him, Porphyras moved a leg, an arm, lifted his head, and opened his eyes.

"Where are you hurt?"

The question did not seem to reach him. In spite of the sharp pain increasing in his right shoulder, he once more tried to get up, and said:

"The tire! The tire! There isn't a nail in it?"

And he fell back groaning, on his side.

Mina, radiant, came to find her brother.

"Porphyras! Good news! Papa is willing!"

Porphyras opened his eyes very wide. "You're sure?"

"Mother and Papa Christophore have been talking it over. Papa was a bit reluctant at first, but in the end he gave in. You can have it when you like."

"Oh, Mina! Truly?"

His face lit up. In spite of the pain in his arm, still sharp enough to be uncomfortable, he started jigging about for joy. Then, seized with sudden doubt, for it was too good to be true, he said: "Is it really sure?"

"As sure as your arm getting broken by a car on the highroad. Papa has even asked Mother whether she can find a dressmaker in Simitra."

That clinched it. It was true. Porphyras began jumping up and down again, without a thought for his broken arm.

"You see, Mina, my nails did help, after all."

For two days, Porphyras buzzed around his mother like

21

a bee around a grape, until she finally agreed to take him to Simitra.

Mina, of course, accompanied them. It was October now, one of the most beautiful months of the year in Greece; for the light from the sky, so much less harsh than at the height of summer, cast shadows that were subtler and purer than at any other time. Porphyras, momentarily forgetting the reason for their journey to the village, said to his sister:

"No wonder so many foreigners come here; it's the most beautiful country in the world!"

"The most beautiful country in the world!" repeated Mina, who, like Porphyras, had never seen any other.

They were walking along together, hand in hand, ahead of their mother, to force her to hurry, but when they reached the summit of the steep cedar-lined slope that twisted and turned as it plunged down into Simitra, they came to a sudden halt.

"There, Mina—see? That's the very place . . . I didn't realize the car was so near . . . I couldn't remember where I was any more. If only you'd seen those great eyes rushing at me . . . I didn't even have time to feel afraid."

This was the first time he had passed the spot since the accident: his injury had kept him at home for a long time.

"Well, we did," said the little girl. "We were terribly afraid. When they brought you home, you looked whiter than goat's milk."

"Pooh!" said Porphyras, in a nonchalant sort of way. "Women always get upset for no reason at all. As it's turned out, everything's absolutely wonderful."

He had already forgotten how he had howled like a banshee when his arm was set, how for thirty-five days he had groused and grumbled about it being imprisoned in a plaster cast. All that belonged to the past. Porphyras was one of those happy souls who only remember pleasant things.

In this case, the pleasant thing was his luck in being hit by such a fine car; he might so easily have been run over by some smuggler's old jalopy that drove on without stopping. The occupants of this car were well-to-do business folk from the plain of Thessaly. They were so shattered by the accident they had brought about that, although they were not wholly responsible for it, they had paid compensation to Porphyras' parents. For those poverty-stricken parents living on the barren soil of Epirus, the amount represented a tidy sum.

So Porphyras, as soon as he was well again, had once more put forward the famous gasoline pump project. His mother would obviously have preferred to use the money on repairing the house, since it was falling to bits; but Papa Christophore was just as eager as his son to have a gasoline pump. He was much less enthusiastic, though, when Porphyras, timidly at first and then with increasing insistence, started talking about certain red overalls seen in front of the service station at Janina.

"Look here, Porphyras, you don't really want to look like a scarecrow?"

"But, Papa Christophore, since at Janina . . ."

"We're not in Janina, Porphyras, and red attracts frogs, not cars!"

Whenever his father became ironic, it was better to give up. But Porphyras was incapable of really yielding. Since no one had ever got anything from Papa Christophore by frontal attack, he must persuade his mother to help him, and, still more important, Mina, who seemed able to coax her father into anything by gently kissing his cheek . . . and in effect Mina had won the battle.

So he was in fact going to have the red uniform of a tiptop garage hand. It was a wonderful world and Greece was a beautiful country.

"You'll see," he said to Mina as they walked on again, "I'll look so magnificent you won't know me . . . and even Papa won't dare tease me!"

They came to the village, with its old white stone and

23

discolored roofs. At last, after a long search in the alleys and sidestreets, they climbed a stairway on which great thick-leaved plants grew in stone jars. This was the dressmaker's house. Porphyras made a face; he would have preferred an expensive shop. Bales of cloth were piled on shelves. The dressmaker showed them everything she had. None of the material was scarlet enough to suit Porphyras. Soon the table and the tiled floor were strewn with cloth; but he only shook his head.

The dressmaker finally managed to discover, at the back of a cupboard, an odd length of so vivid a color that it hit you in the eye like a sunburst.

"That's the one! That's it!" yelled Porphyras in delight.

It was a remnant left over from the time when soldiers of the Greek army wore short scarlet coats. The dressmaker pointed out that the cloth was half eaten by moths, and that it would be extremely difficult to fill in all the holes.

"That's the one! That's it!" was all Porphyras would say.

Mina approved: she never had any doubts about her brother's excellent taste. The dressmaker unrolled the short remnant. Unfortunately there was not enough for a whole uniform with a cap as well.

"I could make you the tunic and trousers," said the dressmaker, "but not the cap. Or the cap but not the trousers."

Cruel dilemma. Porphyras thought it over. Which was the more important? In his mind's eye he saw, one after the other, a soldier, a mailman, a stationmaster, and a policeman. There was no doubt at all that the cap made the man. He asked for the cap, and Mina approved his choice. The dressmaker began to take his measurements.

One week later, Porphyras brought his uniform home in triumph. All the family were called together to see him parading in front of the mirror in the kitchen, in spite of his slight apprehension in case Papa Christophore should tease. But his father only smiled, so Porphyras was able to abandon himself wholeheartedly to his delight.

24

4

The uniform ready, there remained the setting up of the gasoline pump.

One day two village workmen arrived with picks and shovels and sacks of cement. They began to dig a pit. Porphyras never moved an inch away from them: he passed tools, carted earth away, poured drinks for the workmen, looked into the hole that would soon contain the precious fluid brought by a tank wagon as big as a house. Mina followed him everywhere, and listened to his explanations. In two days the pit was dug and cemented. It was in the form of a large cube about six feet deep. Porphyras worked out in his head the distance a car would travel on the amount of gasoline contained in it. He discovered that the car could go around the world. He thought he must be mistaken: it was too stupendous. He went over his calculations three times. There was no mistake.

That evening, at suppertime, his sister went to look for him, since he had not returned to the house. She found him standing on the plank that covered the pit. He was holding

25

an old inner tube from a bicycle as if it were a hose, and talking to invisible people.

"How many, sir? I, Porphyras Patagos, garage hand of the magnificent Patagos Service Station, I can enable you to go right around the world in one lap. Yes, sir, right around. Open all your tanks. Shall we say two hundred and fifty gallons, then? Good-bye, sir, and I hope you have a good journey. Perhaps you would be good enough to greet the Zulus for me, in the name of Porphyras Patagos."

A shout of laughter from Mina interrupted his gasoline sale; but he could not be angry with his sister.

Porphyras' excitement reached such a peak that it infected the whole household. Everyone forgot the nasty accident that could so easily have had tragic consequences. Papa Christophore, for his part, was won over entirely by his son's enthusiasm. The gasoline pump, even though it was not yet set up, took on from day to day an unbelievable importance. The family began to believe that in the future they would be able to live at ease. Porphyras, his tongue between his teeth, was making placards. He put them all over the cedars, on both sides of the house. *Gasoline—Two Miles Ahead* . . . *Gasoline—One Mile Ahead* . . . *Gasoline —Half a Mile Ahead* . . . *Gasoline—Three Hundred Yards Ahead.* He used up a whole can of paint on them. Cars could not fail to stop. In fact, the ones whizzing along neighboring roads would be only too glad to go a little out of their way for the privilege of filling up at the handsome Patagos Service Station.

It was a dream; and life is cruel to dreams, seeking only to destroy them. As they say in Epirus, dreams are kites and life tries to cut the cord that holds them.

One evening, Porphyras was on his way back with his empty milk can, pretending that he was pumping gallon after gallon of gasoline, when suddenly he halted. In the deepening dusk he thought he saw a moving shadow. He could not have said for certain whether it was man or beast, but he was quite sure that the shadow had moved. Without waiting to find out what it was, he broke into a run and raced down the road. For the rest of his journey, he forgot to count his gallons of gasoline. When he got home, he lost no time in telling Mina what he had seen on the highroad.

"It was so queer, Mina. I was really scared."

Mina listened carefully and seemed very troubled. Almost at once she said:

"Porphyras—I've been frightened too."

"Have you been seeing moving shadows?"

"No. But while I was turning the grapes that are drying on the terrace, I saw the first swallow of autumn. She flew around her nest for ages before she perched on it, as though she was afraid to come back to her own home. Then she flew off crying, and she hasn't come back. Mother says it's a bad omen. . . . What does that mean, Porphyras?"

"They say it's a bad sign." Then he added, "You mustn't believe in bad signs, Mina, any more than I should believe in shadows that move. Just think about the dress you'll be having when the gasoline pump is set up. What color will you choose?"

"Red, with white flowers, and birds . . ."

"Well, then, just think hard about your dress."

Forgetting her worries, Mina fell asleep that night dreaming of flowers and birds: while Porphyras, for his part, went back to selling gallon after gallon of gasoline. A few weeks before, together with their big brother Constantine, they had gone back to their attic bedroom, for the nights grew cold near dawn. Porphyras was busily employed with his pump when an unusual noise woke him with a start. Something odd had just happened in the house, and this time he was not imagining things. Constantine and Mina had both given a jump. Below them, their parents were whispering together.

"What is it?" said Mina, terrified.

Constantine struck a light and looked around the loft.

27

Suddenly he began laughing as he pointed to a picture frame leaning against the wall in a shower of broken glass. It was a picture of Papa Christophore in the uniform of a sailor of the Greek fleet, taken twenty years before.

"Only a nail that's given way. It's nothing. Go to sleep again." But as he was going back to his pallet, he saw another small picture, equally shattered, at the foot of the opposite wall.

"I'm scared," said Mina, "I'm scared."

Constantine shrugged his shoulders, and, to reassure her, explained the double fall. "It's only the damp; it's softened the plaster . . . go to sleep again."

The loft was plunged in darkness once more. For his sister's sake, Porphyras pretended to go to sleep, snoring a little; but he too was disturbed. He thought of the shadow he had seen on the road, of the swallow that would not come back to nest beneath the eaves. When at last he fell asleep again, he went on dreaming about cans of gasoline; but this time they would not stand straight, and they fell over, no matter what he did to keep them steady. So he sent them rolling down the hillside with mighty kicks and then slept peacefully until morning.

5

At last the pump was due to arrive. A letter, delivered that very morning by the Simitra mailman, brought the news. Porphyras hoped that it would be as scarlet as his uniform.

Papa Christophore removed the planks that covered the cistern, to see whether the cement had hardened properly. He was taken aback when he saw a long crack splitting one whole side of the pit. He began calling upon all the gods of Olympus to witness the dishonesty and incompetence of the workmen. Then he fell silent, and stood for a long time deep in thought, scratching his head.

"What's up?" Porphyras asked sharply.

His father did not know what answer to make.

"After all, maybe it's not their fault."

"Why, Papa Christophore?"

The father shrugged his shoulders, opened his mouth as though to speak, but said nothing. Porphyras did not insist. He had climbed into the pit, and was running his finger along the crack. There was one place where he could have

29

put his thumb in. Perhaps the workmen were bad, but even so . . .

"Porphyras," his father said, "get off to Simitra at once, find the workmen, and tell them to come back here right away with two bags of their best cement."

"Right, Papa Christophore. I'll fly faster than a swallow!"

He set off for Simitra. It was November. The fields still wore their parched summer look, for the autumn rains were late in coming. The sun still sent warm rays over Epirus, and high among the mountains the somber forests were awaiting their first powdering of snow. The sky was cloudless. Porphyras had every reason in the world to feel carefree, yet something was bothering him. He could not stop thinking about the crack in the cistern, the way his father had shaken his head, looking anxious, the two pictures that had both fallen to the floor the other night, the swallow's terrified cry that Mina had heard.

He was taking the shortcut to avoid the endless winding of the cedar slope when he thought he heard a distant growl of thunder. Was it possible? Thunder when the sky was so clear? Where would a storm come from? Perhaps it was guns fired by soldiers at Arta. No, it couldn't be that, either, the maneuvers had finished three weeks before. What then?

"What nonsense!" he said to himself. "I'm getting scarier than a lizard. It's only the quarrymen on the hillside letting off a charge of dynamite."

Deciding on that sensible explanation, he continued on his way. When he came to Simitra, he discovered that the workmen were off on a job somewhere else and would not be back until noon. Papa Christophore had told him to be sure to see the workmen himself, to explain what had happened and persuade them to return with him immediately. He waited, but at half-past twelve the workmen had still not come back. He made the wife of one of them promise to see to it for him, and then set off for home.

He knew that his family, at that hour of the day, would

be eating; but since his errand was done, there was no need to hurry. Porphyras often went without a meal for the pleasure of loitering by the way. The road passed close by an old pottery factory that had fallen into ruin, separated from the wayside by a dry stone wall. A whole stretch of this wall had fallen down.

"That's queer," he thought. "It was standing all right when I came down not long ago."

And then he began to laugh.

"That was lucky! I might have been there at the wrong moment, and got it on my head."

Stones had rolled to the middle of the road, and he picked them all up. Since his little effort with the nails, he was full of concern for cars. Besides, there was no need now for accidents. The mighty Patagos Service Station would grow rich without them.

In the distance, far behind him, he heard one o'clock striking. "At home they will be having their cheese," he said to himself. "Oh well, never mind!" and did not bother to hasten his step. He had nearly reached the summit of the steep slope, still thinking of the wall that had tumbled down, when suddenly the ground gave way beneath his feet: it was as though his body received a terrific electric charge. He staggered and fell heavily to the ground, his heart gripped with a terrible pain. The blood drained from his face and he began to tremble, not daring to make any attempt to get up. Almost at the same moment the whole countryside moaned, as if a devastating storm were about to break, in spite of the cloudless sky. The moaning lasted a long time, echoing back from the mountains, while near at hand the leaves of the cedars went on shaking frenziedly.

He turned his head at the sound of falling stone; the rest of the wall was crumbling.

Now he understood. It was an earthquake. Pictures flashed through his mind. Things that had puzzled him became clear: the two fallen pictures in the loft, the reluctant swal-

31

low, and above all, the crack in the cistern. The earth was shaking . . . perhaps it would go on shaking, split open before him, and swallow him up.

There were two or three more mighty heavings, followed by distant rumblings, and the same quivering of the leaves. Then they grew less. At that moment Porphyras came to himself. He thought of his home, of Mina. She must be terrified out of her wits about him. He must set her mind at rest.

With great difficulty he got to his feet. His legs would hardly hold him up, although he was not in the least hurt, not even a scratch. He touched his icy cheeks. No, he was not hurt at all, and yet the pain stayed with him.

His heart thudding, he set off for home. Turning to look toward Simitra, hidden at the bottom of the slope, he saw a tall column of black smoke rising steadily into the tranquil sky. The whole countryside had suddenly plunged again into a terrifying silence: no more chirping of grasshoppers, no birdsong, nothing any more but a great stillness.

He began to run across the fields; uprooted olive trees were lying like dead bodies on the ground. As he drew near home, an inward fear increased his agony. He climbed a small mound to see the house sooner—and stood rooted to the spot. Instead of the house, he could see only a shapeless heap of broken stones, and from them slowly rose, like smoke, a fine white dust. A little farther on, by the side of the road, the magnificent Patagos Service Station was in a similar condition. No sound, no voice, came from the shambles. Only a solitary swallow circled above, uttering sharp cries of terror.

Porphyras, his face distorted, stood there paralyzed, looking with eyes grown haggard. Then a great cry of horror burst from him. Beside himself with terror, he fled at breakneck speed across the dead countryside.

6

For the first time in weeks it was raining.
The marketplace at Timiza, once a large empty square, was now a canvas village: more than fifty tents had been hastily set up, great dark masses streaming with cascades of water. It was as though the rain had only waited for the disaster before coming to finish off the unhappy country. And in addition to all this, the weather was rather cold.

At one end of the square, one of the biggest tents was marked with a red cross. Two women in white uniforms had just gone inside. Walking to the far end, they halted by a row of straw mattresses. One of them pointed.

"This is the child."

"Which one?"

"The one asleep."

"You still don't know where he came from?"

"He's asleep most of the time. And when he's awake, he seems dazed."

"No one has recognized him?"

"No one. He certainly doesn't live in Timiza."

"Still, he was found here. He must have been here when it happened. I suppose he's already been questioned?"

"He's not very alert when he's awake: he doesn't seem to understand. The boy next to him says he has nightmares about falling cans and gasoline catching fire. It's possible that his house went up in flames, like so many others."

"Yet he doesn't seem to have any burns."

"No. It's his mind that is affected. He's trying to blot out what happened."

The two women leaned over the child sleeping there peacefully in spite of the noise of the rain drumming on the canvas. Then they moved on, stopping by other victims stretched out on pallets or crouching on the floor itself. There were roughly thirty people in the tent, boys and men of all ages, some with bandaged heads, others with an arm in a sling or a leg in plaster. The pungent smell of medical dressings, ether, and iodine hung about the tent, heavy and sickening. Every face showed the same anguish, the same grief, the same hopelessness, the same resignation. And the same desolate sight could be seen in the fifty other tents. Little, if anything, was left of the small town of Timiza. Three hundred houses were completely destroyed and the others rendered uninhabitable, while hundreds of people had been killed and thousands injured. And Timiza was not the only place to suffer. Philas, Marissa, Simitra had been badly hit, Simitra worst of all. In it there were not ten walls left standing. In the space of a few seconds the whole of that part of Epirus, already desolate, had become a wasteland.

But Porphyras knew nothing of this. For three days he had slept, as though to put off a terrible awakening for as long as possible.

Yet that awakening was drawing near, stealing silently upon him like a jackal, prowling sometimes so close that it almost brushed against that little dark head.

Then one night he stopped putting the gasoline cans

35

straight, and began thinking about the crack in the cistern, and the workmen . . . yes, of course, the workmen . . . the workmen. That reminded him of something . . . what was it? Of course, he had gone to Simitra to fetch them. But why hadn't he returned home? Why?

He repeated the word "Why?" several times over.

Suddenly he sat bolt upright on his mattress. His ears, until then deaf to the world, heard the sound of the rain on the tent. He looked around in astonishment. He was

filled with a frenzy of terror. At the top of his voice he screamed—"Mama! Mama!"

A lady in a white uniform ran up to him and took him in her arms as though he were a baby. He gave way to his grief; big tears rolled down his cheeks.

"Where's Mama? Where's Mina?"

The nurse said nothing, only went on holding him in her arms. She rocked him gently for a long time; then she said softly:

"Who are you, my dear? Where do you come from? What's your name?"

His name? What name? He could not remember. Did he ever have a name? Ah yes, he thought he heard his mother call him "my little Porphyras." Porphyras, that's who he was.

"Porphyras Patagos," he sighed, looking up into the face leaning over him.

"What village?"

"It's called Simitra."

"Simitra? But that's over five miles away."

"I live at the top of the long cedar slope. There's a garage there—the big Patagos Service Station, you must know it. . . ."

The nurse had never heard of the Patagos Service Station, but she pretended to know it.

"And how did you get here?"

Yes, how? That was another vast gap in his memory. He thought as hard as he could, but it was no good.

"Try to remember. You were found here in Timiza. Why did you come here?"

The nurse tried to help him to remember. Then suddenly the gap was bridged. Once more he looked upon the terrible sight of his home in ruins, saw again his panic-stricken flight across the desolate fields, stumbling and falling until he dropped with exhaustion in front of the outlying devastated houses of a strange town. He screamed again:

"Mama! Mama!"

It was horrifying to hear him. Merciful sleep had kept the truth from him for three days, but now there was no escape.

"Mama? Where is she? And Mina? . . . And Papa Christophore? . . . Constantine?"

He did not ask if they were alive, but it was clear that that was what he meant. The nurse nodded her head. She wanted to reassure him, but she dared not lie.

"We'll soon know, my dear."

38

"I want to go home. They're expecting me. I want to go now."

"Listen to the rain pelting down. . . . And you're not strong enough yet. You haven't eaten a thing for three days; you must get your strength back first. Would you like something to drink?"

"I'm terribly thirsty."

The lady in the white uniform went away and was back almost at once with a mug of milk. Porphyras tasted it, and made a face.

"I'm afraid, my dear, it's not goat's milk."

His thirst made him overcome his dislike. He emptied the mug in long gulps, as if it were medicine.

"May I have some more? I'm so thirsty."

Gradually his head cleared. Thoughts went round and round like the sails of a windmill in the Sicilian winds. His eyes, until then blank and unfocused, became aware of the tent and the unhappy people it sheltered. There was an old man sitting with his head in his hands, as still and silent as though he'd been turned to stone; beyond him a small boy was cuddling a plush rabbit; somewhere a child was crying. Porphyras knew why, and he too began to cry.

As it was, he had to spend a whole night among these groans and tears before he learned the truth. The nurse had promised to come back as soon as she could. The terrible night of waiting seemed endless, for he was no longer able to sleep. Mama . . . Papa . . . Mina . . . Constantine? What had become of them?

Dawn light was filtering into the tent when at last the lady in the white uniform reappeared. She was no longer smiling as she had been the day before, and she looked troubled. The boy flung himself upon her.

"Mama! . . . Oh, tell me quickly! Quickly!"

The nurse did not speak. She turned her face away; then she said:

"A truck is leaving for Simitra with a load of mattresses.

It will take you along. . . . Do you feel well enough to go?"

Outside, the rain had stopped, but great gray clouds of mourning sailed across the beautiful sky of Greece. Porphyras looked at the canvas tents pitched higgledy-piggledy in the public square, and then at the broken, crumbling walls of the town beyond.

The truck was waiting, crammed with an enormous pile of mattresses. The nurse whispered a few words in the driver's ear. Porphyras would have liked to know what she said, but he did not try to overhear. The driver swung the boy up in his arms into the seat beside his own, and the heavy truck set off. Porphyras' heart sank. He wanted to talk, to ask questions; but his mouth would not open. He was afraid of the truth.

The journey seemed endless; but at last he saw "Simitra" on a signpost. It couldn't be true! The village he had visited so many times before was not recognizable. He began to tremble again. An abrupt turn to the right, another to the left, and the truck drew up in the public square, where dark tents loomed against the sky, just as they had at Timiza.

"Stay here and wait until someone comes," said the driver, getting down from the cab.

Porphyras obeyed, but his eyes never left the man as he walked off rapidly. Where was the driver going? Time stood still. Why couldn't he get down?

At last the man came back, together with a lady dressed in white, like the one at Timiza. She, too, was smiling, but with the sort of smile he was beginning to know, terrifying and not reassuring at all.

"Get down now, dear. Give me your hand."

"Where are you taking me?"

No reply. He let himself be taken down. They walked along, side by side, in silence.

"Your name is Patagos, isn't it?"

"Porphyras Patagos."

"And you used to live in that little farm at the top of the cedar slope?"

He nodded.

"You had a sister called Marina?"

"A sister, and my brother Constantine . . . and Mama and Papa Christophore."

The nurse received this avalanche of names in silence. They were walking slowly through the tents, too slowly: the slowness was a bad sign. Porphyras knew that good news travels fast. From time to time the nurse sighed; then she put her hand on his head.

"You're almost grown up, aren't you, Porphyras? And you're brave."

He looked at her sadly, and even pitifully, knowing that she was tormented by what she could not bring herself to tell him . . . For he understood now. Two years before, his mother had taken him aside in exactly the same way, to tell him of the death of his other little sister, Myrtha, from a snake bite.

They had come to a big circular tent, that looked like the one belonging to the soldiers who had been on maneuvers in those parts some weeks before.

"Porphyras," the nurse said abruptly, holding both his hands. "I must tell you the truth: a very sad truth. You won't see your mother or your father or your big brother again—but your little sister . . ."

Each one of those names had pierced his heart as though someone had put a knife through it, but at the last he lifted his head.

"Mina! Mina! She's alive?"

The nurse pointed to the tent.

"She's in there . . . you'll find it difficult to recognize her. Her head's all covered with bandages. She was hurt, but not seriously. She'll soon be well."

"Mina! Mina! Oh, I must see her!"

The nurse lifted the flap. He began to tremble all over. Eagerly his eyes searched the semidarkness that lay within the tent.

"Porphyras! Porphyras!"

The familiar little voice made him jump, and he turned around. Oh no, he would never have recognized his sister, so pale beneath the bandages that swallowed up most of her face. But her voice could not be mistaken. He rushed toward her, clasped her in his arms, and both of them burst into tears.

7

It was a big dormitory, as long as a street, feebly lit by the night lights in the ceiling, with dozens and dozens of beds ranged in three rows. And in each of these beds was an orphan.

More than three hundred of them were living in the old barracks that had been transformed into a Home: the girls in one wing, the boys in the other. They had been moved there, to Lyssira in Thessaly, until something better turned up.

In that dormitory, Porphyras' bed was the fifth on the right as you came in. His bed was like all the rest, except for the view of Simitra, cut from a newspaper, that he had fastened to its head. The boy on his left was from Timiza: Porphyras had met him first in the tent, and then had come upon him by accident a few days later. His name was Zaïmis, and he was thirteen, a few months older than Porphyras. He had been dragged from the ruins of his home with a slight leg wound, which had already healed. Like Porphyras, he would never see his mother or father again.

43

His grief was pitiful to see, for nothing would console him. He was not alone in the world, however. The disaster had spared him a sister and a grandfather. Both were at the moment in a hospital, but he would rejoin them later. It was nearly always at night that his loss became unendurable. After lights out, he would burrow beneath his bedclothes, and Porphyras could hear him sobbing. Porphyras would stretch out to take the boy's hand in his own.

"Don't cry, Zaïmis, don't cry, I'm here . . . I've just been looking at the sky, it's all filled with stars. It'll be fine to-morrow, so they're sure to take us for a walk."

Every night Porphyras found something pleasant that Zaïmis could look forward to on the following day, and every night he succeeded in calming his grief, until in the end Zaïmis fell asleep, still holding his friend's hand.

In the morning, when he woke up, very much ashamed of his weakness of the night before, he would turn to Porphyras and smile his thanks.

One day he said to him: "It's queer, Porphyras, you seem to be happy, in spite of everything, while I shall always be miserable."

"I'm not happy, Zaïmis."

"Well, you enjoy the games they organize to cheer us up; I often hear you laughing. And whenever a truck comes down the street and stops in front of the garage, you always climb up to the window to look at it, and I can see then that you're happy."

Porphyras was astounded, and just a little hurt. It was quite possible to be deeply unhappy and yet still feel like laughing sometimes. The two things were quite different. Every time he thought of his home, his heart bled; and he knew why his face had grown thinner . . . but his home was not only Mama, Papa Christophore, Constantine: it was also the fields that smelled so good, that would always be scented with thyme and savory and lavender; it was Mina, who was all he had and whom he must keep safe

44

from all harm. And now there was Zaïmis too, whom he would never have known except for the catastrophe. Certain people, certain things, were dead: other things, other people, were alive, and he was one of them.

But how could he explain these complicated matters to Zaïmis, when he felt instinctively that he was right, without being able to express his thoughts? He knew that he must not give way to grief. Mina, and Zaïmis as well, needed him. There was no harm in keeping a zest for life.

One morning Zaïmis said: "I wish we could be together always. But . . ." He pointed to the empty bed nearest Porphyras on the left, then to another a little farther away, then a third.

"Perhaps I'll never get away!" sighed Porphyras. Then, looking at his friend, he added, "I'd rather stay here."

For some time now gaps had been appearing in the dormitories. The extent of the damage had brought about, in Greece and in many other countries, a tremendous feeling of brotherhood. Hundreds of letters poured into Athens. Offers of hospitality, particularly for orphans, came from all quarters of the globe. A ship had already set out for Turkey. There was talk as well of the northern countries.

"Since you and your sister have no folk any more, you're bound to go," sighed Zaïmis. "Would you like to go to a foreign land?"

"I don't know. I'd like to travel, but only if I could be sure of coming back. Some foreigners stopped at our garage once, in Simitra. They'd come from a long way away, from Norway, I think. They could speak a little Greek. While Papa Christophore was doing the repairs, they looked at the scenery around Epirus. They kept looking up at the sky and saying they'd never seen so clear a sky anywhere. I could see they weren't saying it just to please us, they were much too delighted. Well, I feel like that about our sky, Zaïmis; I wouldn't want to lose it; I'm glad I'm Greek."

"So am I, Porphyras."

They talked together every morning and every evening, when they got up and when they went to bed. But for Porphyras the best hours of the day were those spent with Mina. He had always been extremely attached to his sister. Now she was all the family he had, and he felt that he had a special duty toward her. It was his job now to look after her, and the responsibility was at once heavy and welcome. Mina returned his affection with all her heart. It was her love for her brother that had saved her life. Just before the terrible earthquake that razed Epirus to the ground, she was having a meal. Anxious about her brother's long absence, she had risen from the table and rushed out to see if he was coming. The cataclysm came upon her as she stood by the garage, and a tile had cut into her face.

Porphyras was able to see his sister every day in a court-yard that formed part of the barracks. There they told each other all the little bits of news going around the Home, talked about Simitra, or else fell silent, quietly enjoying the pleasure of being together.

On this particular afternoon, Porphyras hardly knew his sister. He had grown used to seeing her in the big white bandage that went around her head and beneath her chin; and now it was all off, and there was only a small crisscross dressing near her temple.

"Look!" she said. "Does the scar show much? Do you think it will always be there?"

"I can hardly see it, Mina."

"Do I look just as I did before?"

He hesitated, then said: "Yes, exactly."

It was not quite true: it would probably never be true. The scar made a long weal that would never completely disappear. But Porphyras knew that girls thought a lot about their looks, and he did not want to upset her.

"I'm sure it will soon disappear."

The little girl smiled, reassured. Then she said: "Good; then I won't be so ugly for the journey."

Porphyras frowned.

"What journey?"

"Oh, haven't they told you? We're leaving, Porphyras. I don't know where we're going, except that it's very far away. We were called into the office. They said we'd be very much happier than we are here . . . everyone would spoil us . . . But why aren't you pleased, Porphyras? Don't you want to go?"

He nodded.

"Are you sure we're both going? No one's said anything to me. When did they tell you?"

"This morning, after breakfast."

Porphyras questioned his sister further; then, seeing the matron, he went straight up to her.

"Is it true that we're leaving?" he said breathlessly.

The matron's smile faded. Porphyras' heart sank as she put her arm around his shoulders and drew him to her.

"I am going with Mina, aren't I?"

"I'm afraid not, dear. Very few families, you see, are willing to take two children. And then, you are big and strong, you'll soon be ready to earn your living. You can stay in Greece."

"Mina wouldn't want to go without me."

"I know she'll be unhappy at first. But she'll soon settle down all right. She needs a lot of building up, your little sister. Haven't you noticed her pale cheeks and the dark shadows under her eyes? And of course you'll be able to write to each other as much as you like."

Mina came to join them. The matron turned to the little girl.

"You want to go, don't you?"

Mina understood. Her head bowed, she stood there crying silently.

"Have you really changed your mind?"

The little girl's sole reply was to cling desperately to her brother's arm and hide her face against him. The matron

47

went on:

"Look, Porphyras, you're a big boy now, and you must try to understand. It won't be a long separation. It's only for a few months, and it's for your sister's good, for the sake of her health. Marina will come back to you with rosy cheeks and a good appetite. It will be easier for her to forget what has happened when she is away from here."

Shaken, Porphyras looked from the matron to his sister. He did not speak.

"Obviously," the matron insisted, making her point, "we can't always do as we like. In any case, Marina won't be leaving for a few days: you'll have time to get used to the idea. From now on, you'll have permission to be with each other for a longer time each day."

She went off smiling. Porphyras and Mina stood there side by side, hand in hand. Without speaking, they walked to the big yew tree at the far end of the yard, so that they could be alone. In spite of the cold, they sank down on a stone bench. Mina put her head on her brother's knees, and suddenly burst out crying.

"I don't want to, Porphyras, I don't want to!"

The poor boy had no idea what to do or what to say to comfort her.

"Don't think about it any more, Mina. We've several days ahead of us, and we shall be seeing more of each other."

When the bell rang, they found it hard to separate, and the eyes of both were red-rimmed.

That night, bed number five in the dormitory was the center of a great sorrow. For a long time Porphyras wept beneath the bedclothes. Then Zaïmis stretched out a hand to comfort his friend.

"Don't cry, Porphyras—Mina hasn't gone yet . . . Who knows what may happen in the next few days?"

The following day, Porphyras found his sister very pale, and the day after that, paler still. She would die of grief if she went. Taking his courage in both hands, he approached

48

the matron again, and this time she was not so gentle with him. She accused him of working on his sister's feelings. The decision had been made; nothing could be done about it.

He went away, with his head bowed, and that night bed number five was again shaken by his weeping.

Porphyras always reacted quickly. If nothing could be done, the best thing was to forget it at once. But when something could be done . . . and it *could!*

"Oh!" said Zaïmis, when Porphyras told him his plan. "You can't do that!"

"I will not allow my sister to be taken away from me. Grown-ups seem to think they can arrange everything to suit themselves. Anyway, Zaïmis, don't be surprised if tomorrow night my bed stays empty."

"You mean to . . . to . . . ?"

"To go off with Mina."

"Where?"

"I don't want her to leave me."

"It's bad to go off like that, to run away."

"I'm not really running away. I only want Mina to stay with me. We'll go and hide somewhere. And when the train's gone, we'll come back."

Every afternoon, weather permitting, the young refugees of Epirus were taken for a walk, the boys going one way, the girls another. Once in the country, they were allowed to run where they liked. It would not be difficult to escape. That was what Porphyras had decided to do. Mina as well. For their meeting place he fixed upon the ruins of an old temple on the hillside looking over Lyssira.

Porphyras watched the sky the whole of that morning. The evening before the sky had clouded over, and a few raindrops had fallen in the yard. But in Greece the sky is never overcast for very long. From the heights of Olympus the benevolent god Zeus sends squadrons to sweep it clear of the gray clouds. It would be fine today.

After their meal, the children assembled in the yard

and set off at once. The boys, in a long line, went through the village streets. Porphyras never even thought of staring at the service stations and the gasoline pumps, as he normally did. He thought only of his sister. He was walking in the rear with Zaïmis, and they were holding hands.

"So that's understood, Zaïmis; you won't say a word, since we'll be coming back."

"I won't say a word . . . but I'll be thinking of you all the time."

It so happened that they were taken to the ilex woods south of the village, near the quarries.

"You see, Zaïmis—you must admit I'm always lucky!"

When they came to the thickets, the children disbanded. The quarries were riddled with hiding places. Porphyras shook hands warmly with his friend, hugged him unobtrusively, and disappeared. As soon as he thought he was out of sight, he began to run as fast as he could through the undergrowth, avoiding the paths and goat tracks. Half an hour later he arrived, out of breath, within sight of the crumbling columns of the temple of Helios, standing like ancient torches among the rocks.

Mina had not yet come. There was nothing surprising in that, for the girls had set out after the boys. They always forgot something or other at the last moment. And then, Mina couldn't run as fast as he could. He sat down on one of the marble slabs roughened by the depredations of centuries. He was free and happy. And since he was free and happy, he began to think of the barracks in which he had been living for the last three weeks. Porphyras was like that. He only realized that he had been unhappy when it was all over and, by comparison, found himself contented with his lot. How wonderful it was to discover another horizon, so wide, so blue, the beautiful Grecian countryside hardly touched by winter's icy fingers.

For a long time he stared at the misty blue horizon, until it seemed to him that behind the distant hills there was yet

50

another that for a long time had been hidden by shadows: his own special horizon, where he would be able to sell gasoline.

He had come back to his gasoline pumps. They were, for Porphyras, the buoys that always remain afloat in spite of shipwreck. Hands are stretched out to them: not everyone reaches them, but right to the very end they offer hope. Sitting on the marble slabs gilded by the winter sun, he began to dream again of his red overalls. He did not regret the uniform that lay among the ruins of his home. He found it pleasant now to dwell upon the moth holes, the tarnished buttons, and the missing trousers. The overalls he intended to have later would be very much better.

Time goes quickly spent in thought . . . quicker still in dreaming. Porphyras was startled to see the shadows of the great yews climbing across the marble flagstones, to feel the cold air creeping down his neck. He got to his feet and scanned the deserted hillside. No reason for worry yet. The girls must have gone to the other side of the village, and that would mean a wide detour for Mina. Unless . . . no, he knew Mina; she wanted to be with him so much that she would be careful to choose the right moment for her escape.

He tried to lose himself again in his vision of service stations and gasoline pumps, but he found it very difficult. He was seized by a nagging fear. It is true that in Greece the winter sun keeps nearly all its summer heat; but the nights make up for it. He shivered under the malicious touch of a breeze sharp as a green lemon. Still Mina did not come. With all his strength he rejected the thought that at that very moment she was going through the village with the others, on her way back to the Home.

"I'll count up to a thousand," he told himself. And he began to count, tapping with the toe of his shoe.

The sun threw out a great sheaf of rays like an armful of branches cast on a dying fire, and was extinguished be-

51

hind the mountains. As he had done in the past, Porphyras lifted his eyes to look for the first stars. Those he saw were diamond bright. It would freeze tonight. Anxiety took firmer hold. He saw Mina lost, wandering through the fields, crying out with terror. Yet he still wanted to believe she would come. He risked showing himself on the hillside, shouting, "Mina! Mina!"

The silence of approaching night was absolute. His own voice frightened him. He came back to the marble steps and sat down, shivering with cold. The town, deep in shadow, was a shapeless mass. But soon it shone forth dazzling white. The moon had risen above the mountains of Pindus. A sudden hope shot through him. If it was just that Mina was lost, she would be able to see her way now. He waited. An hour passed. The hard stone drew all the cold of the night; he dared not sit down. Leaning against a column, he stared desperately over the valley.

Midnight bells sounded in the distance. She would not come now. Perhaps, at the end of her endurance, she had collapsed somewhere in the brushwood. Why had he waited so long before running to help her? He stumbled down the hill, to the right, to the left, tripping over the sharp-pointed stones. And suddenly he found himself among houses, on the outskirts of the town. What could he do? The town meant the barracks; he would not go there. Retracing his steps, he looked everywhere for her. But the town, milky white under the moon, drew him back in spite of himself. He ventured into the streets. Every time a shadow fell along the pavement, he flattened himself against a doorway. When the shadow passed, he ran on again, his heart thudding, believing he saw Mina in the distance.

He walked about for a long time, exhaustion dragging at his heels, the cold going right through his clothes. Hunching his shoulders, he wandered on without knowing where he was going, with his elbows pressed close to his sides.

Where was he making for? He went on like a sleepwalker; and maybe he was indeed asleep.

Suddenly he shivered. There rose before him a long wall pierced with windows all exactly alike. His feet had brought him back, unconsciously, to the barracks. His anxiety, numbed by exhaustion, flared up again. Was Mina there, behind that great wall? . . . No, he could no longer wait, he had to know.

The heavy iron gate was securely bolted, and over all hung a dignified silence. He pushed with all his strength, but he no longer had any strength. He had spent it all night long, looking for his sister. Tears, until then resolutely held back, forced their way through his eyelids. Porphyras realized that the little courage he had left was fast ebbing away. He crumpled up against the foot of that high wall, abandoned and overcome with cold.

The porter found him there the following morning when he came out to sweep the pavement. The boy's first words were not for himself, but for his sister:

"Mina? Where is Mina?"

He was carried into the white-painted sanatorium, where a cup of coffee revived him, and there he learned why Mina had not come to meet him on the hillside. Worn out with grief, the little girl had collapsed just as she came out of the refectory. In spite of all her protestations she had been put to bed, and later, when her brother's absence was discovered, she confessed everything.

So Porphyras returned to the Home. He was scolded, but all the same he was forgiven . . . and as it turned out, he got what he wanted. Brother and sister were not to be separated. They would either stay in the Home or leave together.

8

And leave together they did . . . With a smile, this time a beaming smile, the matron broke the news to them. They were going to a distant land that was always green, where everyone was rich, and every child happy. This country had a curious name—it was called Holland. They would travel thousands of miles to get there. A family of peasant folk, like their own, was expecting them, and they would be given every care. Nor were they the only ones to be going so far: a special train would be taking them with other young refugees to this northern country.

"Will there be cars and service stations there, as there are in Greece?" asked Porphyras anxiously.

"Holland is a wealthier country than Greece, Porphyras."

Wealthier! That meant more garages, more gasoline pumps. Wonderful!

It was January now. After several days of cold, gray weather that had placed white caps upon the mountains, old Zeus had renewed his everlasting battle against the clouds. The day they left, the sky regained its exquisite transparency. On the platform, flooded with sunshine, it was as though spring had come. Holding their luggage, Porphyras and Mina waited with Zaïmis, who had been given permission to see them to the train.

"You're lucky to be going," murmured Zaïmis.

"You're lucky to have someone left so that you can stay," Porphyras answered him.

"We'll write to you," promised Mina. "When we come back, we'll tell you everything we've seen."

They said good-bye. The train began to move. Zaïmis went on waving his handkerchief until he could no longer be seen.

"Poor Zaïmis," said Porphyras, putting his own handkerchief back in his pocket. "Tonight, in bed, he'll have no one to hold his hand."

At once, however, the two of them were suddenly made more light-hearted by the change of scene and the excitement of the unknown. Noses pressed against the windows, they devoured these new aspects of their native Greece. Towns flashed by, all white, and glimpses of the sea, all blue. It was a queer experience to reach the frontier, a little station where people no longer spoke as they did, nor wore the same kind of clothes.

The train sped along, rarely stopping. Night came upon the children unawares, as they were traveling beside a wide and tranquil river, very different from the torrents of Epirus or Thessaly. Then they could no longer see the countryside. What fun it was then to be cozily packed in a compartment that was like a warm little house.

They laughed and sang for a long time before they fell asleep, curled up in their seats, rocked by the rapid movement of the train.

When he awoke, Porphyras rubbed his eyes hard, and rushed to the door, stepping over the sleeping bodies. It was dawn. "Snow!" he exclaimed. Turning to the others, he shouted at the top of his voice, "It's snow! Snow!" Everyone rushed to the windows. Snow! It covered everything as far as the flat horizon, where there were no mountains.

"Snow!" sighed Mina. "Is it cold in the country we're going to?"

Then she said, "Oh look—houses! Is this a big town?"

They were in fact coming into a town. The train stopped there quite a while. They were given permission to get out to stretch their legs.

"Brr!" Mina said, huddling up in her coat.

The young refugees had only just got out on the platform when they were surrounded by a crowd of smiling strangers. Hands stretched toward them, offering rolls, buns, cups of coffee, bags of candy. Everyone smiled at them and spoke to them, using strange words, but ones that were obviously friendly.

When the train moved off, Porphyras leaned out of the window to see the name of this big foreign town that was every bit as hospitable as a Greek one. And suddenly he saw enormous scarlet letters on a wooden panel: BELGRADE.

"Of course," he thought. "It's the capital of the great country next to ours."

He was deeply moved at the thought of the people of a great city hundreds of miles from Greece taking such trouble over orphans.

The journey continued, over mountains and across immense plains. It lasted for another two days, two endless days for Mina. They crossed Hungary, Austria, Germany; the little girl was no longer taking anything in. Only, from time to time, looking at the snow, she said, "We're terribly far from home."

At last, on the third morning, a rumor ran from end to end of the train: this was Holland! The children were asked to collect their luggage, and then they got out of the train to find themselves in a big station. The same travelers who had been so light-hearted as they left Greece no longer wanted to laugh, nor even to talk. Separation was upon them. There, in that station, they shook hands with each other for the last time. Each would go a different way, into the homes of strangers speaking an unknown language. Several children were crying.

"How lucky we are," Porphyras said to his sister, "that there are two of us."

They went into a vast room. Officials, seated at desks, called out names . . . the names of the little refugees from Epirus, that they pronounced very queerly. The child named went up to the desk. Sometimes a man, more often a woman, took the boy or girl away. Like the others, Porphyras and his sister were moving along with the line when suddenly a voice called:

"Porphyras Patagos! . . . Marina Patagos!"

They left the line and came forward hesitantly. A very fat woman stood near the desk. She was enormous, her face the color of well-baked Cretan pottery, her hair an even paler gold than maize in Epirus in September.

"I'm scared," Mina whispered, clutching her brother's sleeve.

But the lady was smiling at them; and a smile has the same power in every country in the world. She said something they did not understand, and, taking Mina by the hand, invited them to follow her. Before they went through the door, the two children looked back at the others for the last time, saying farewell with their eyes.

In the new train into which they had climbed, the little orphans remained silent a long time, terribly impressed by the corpulence of the lady. They realized that she wanted to be friendly. She unpacked all sorts of delicacies from a bag she had with her, bent on stuffing the children. Mina found her so entirely different from Greek women she was sure she would never get used to her.

All this while the train was traveling across vast and monotonous plains. There was no more snow, but there

57

seemed to be water everywhere. They crossed rivers so wide that in the end they had to leave the train and go on board ship.

"Where are we going now?" Mina asked in great distress. "Do you think we really are in Holland?"

As a matter of fact, Porphyras was asking himself the same question. Night was falling, bringing no reassurance. The boat sailed along in the darkness for a long time before it came into port. Mina sighed with relief when she found herself on firm land again. A conveyance was drawn up on the quayside: not a car, but a light carriage drawn by an enormous horse with monumental cruppers. A man wearing boots, and enveloped in a transparent raincoat rather like a diving suit, came up to them, took the luggage from the fat woman, with a loud laugh lifted first Porphyras and then Mina into the cart, and set off with them.

The horse's hooves clacked like castanets. Porphyras and Mina, in the back, tucked the rug they had been given around their knees. Mina kept her head down because of the drizzle blowing like a fine mist against them. She did not speak. At that moment she was imagining herself back again on the terrace of her home at Simitra, drying plums in the sun. The sun! They had not seen it once since their departure.

Porphyras, too, was thinking . . . but not only of his own country. He was in Holland, he was eager to learn what was in store for him. "We crossed by boat," he said to himself. "So we're on an island. Will there be cars on an island?" A precise and pertinent question. So that he could give himself an answer, he thought of his own country, of the islands of the Ionian Sea, of Corfu and Cephalonia. . . . They were not very far from his home, and he had often heard about them. He tried to bring these islands back to mind, or rather to imagine them, knee-deep in cars.

The cessation of castanets on the road interrupted his thinking. They had arrived. The man in the diving suit lifted

them down from the cart. A door opened, revealing a hall
that was soaking wet. What an extraordinary country!
thought Porphyras. It rains even inside the houses!

Before entering, the man took off his boots, the fat lady
her shoes, and both put on thick felt slippers.

"Slippers to walk through the wet in!" Porphyras was
astonished again. Now the lady was inviting them in their

59

turn to put on the slippers she was holding out to them. And Porphyras suddenly understood that the tiles were not wet, but polished . . . so highly polished that, as he entered, his right foot slid away from his left, and he found himself upon his seat, closely followed by Mina, who had been foolish enough to give him a hand.

Laughing, the two children were just getting to their feet again when they became aware of two more unknown faces, also laughing heartily.

"Piet! Johanna!" said the fat lady, pointing to the boy and the girl.

"Piet . . . Johanna." Porphyras tried to repeat the names.

"Piet . . . Johanna," murmured Mina.

When the little Greeks had given their own names, the four children stared at each other, amazed to see how different they were. Piet held out his hand, and Porphyras did the same. Johanna, blushing, went up to Mina and kissed her.

The highly polished corridor opened into a big room. Mina felt as though she were entering a palace. Everything —floor, walls, ceiling, and big copper jars—was dazzling bright. She was so afraid of falling, or of dirtying something, that she hardly dared take a step. Yet obviously they were going to have a meal here; for the table was set, and a steaming bowl of soup was already waiting.

During the meal Mina could not take her eyes from the Dutch children, particularly Johanna, whose thick fair braids reminded her of the ropes used by potters in Epirus to tie up their wares. Her pale blue eyes worried Mina. She could not read their expression. She began to think of little Greek girls, her friends at Simitra, and the ones who were with her at Lyssira. Slowly her eyes filled with tears. To have traveled so far only to be unhappy!

Seeing her heavy eyes, the fat lady thought she was half asleep. She indicated that her young charges should come upstairs to bed. The stairs, and the bedrooms too, were polished to a high gloss. It was a miracle that children who nearly all their lives had gone barefoot were able to keep their footing on such a surface. Fortunately, the sheets were not polished! The Dutchwoman was understanding enough to have put both their beds in the same room for that first night.

"*Goede nacht!*" she said as she left them.

That must mean good night. As soon as they were alone, Mina flung herself into her brother's arms, a little lost girl desperately needing help.

"Porphyras! I want . . . I want to go back this very minute!"

"You're tired out, Mina . . . you'll feel better tomorrow . . . and we'll soon learn to stop slipping all over the floors."

The little girl smiled. She snuggled down into her bed, then sighed blissfully . . . her feet had come into contact with the cozy warmth of a hot-water bottle.

"The lady is certainly very kind," she murmured. "Perhaps I'll grow to love her. And you'll be with me always."

9

Three months had gone by. Both Porphyras and Mina had made many discoveries. First, they had learned that as Greece is the country of sunshine, so Holland is the country of water. There is water everywhere in Holland; in the sky, on the earth, in the air you breathe, in the clothes you wear.

"You know," said Mina, "Holland is just like one of those sponges from Corfu soaked in a stream."

She added: "If only it were laughing water!"

By laughing water she meant the water from lively springs, bubbling among rocks and dashing over waterfalls in cascades.

They had learned something else: Dutch was no longer incomprehensible jargon for them. Its words had meaning; they could understand and make themselves understood. Porphyras, gifted with an astonishing memory, could now hold long conversations with his friend Piet van Hoolen, while Mina was content to listen to Johanna.

Piet had taken the young Greeks to explore this curious

land, where people are gay in spite of having no sun; where everything is so hygienic that cows' tails are tied up to the roofs of the cowsheds; where horses have curtains at the windows of their stables; where everyone eats pounds of butter and no one knows the taste of olive oil; where no one has ever heard a grasshopper, yet everyone can imitate the sound on a guitar; where everyone, from the humblest stevedore to the Queen Mother herself, goes about on a bicycle—even including fat Mrs. van Hoolen, with her pale eyes and hair the color of maize. And since everyone in Holland goes about on a bicycle, that was how Porphyras and Mina, together with Piet and Johanna, went to school each morning.

School was an important part of their new life. Every morning, as they arrived, they had to take their shoes off, for the school, too, was highly polished. At school, Dutch children learn to sweep and dust and clean, to polish with oil and beeswax and "elbow grease." Mina and Porphyras did not lose their footing any more. Indeed, Porphyras was expert now in the art of sliding all around a room like a skater, one foot lifted behind him, without knocking into a single piece of furniture.

They liked their school, even though discipline was far more severe than anything they had known in Greece. The main thing was they had very quickly learned that it is as easy to understand blue eyes as dark ones. They stopped being gypsies to be looked at askance, to whom no one would lend a handkerchief for fear it would not be returned. On the register they were simply Mina and Porphyras, as the others were Piet, Johanna, Kees, or Maria.

Their teacher, a tall young girl fresh as a tulip from Marken, obviously liked her new pupils, with just a slight reservation perhaps in the case of Porphyras, whom she found intelligent but a little temperamental. How could this tall young girl possibly understand that Porphyras would never be quite like the others? Sometimes he spoke his thoughts aloud, or suddenly went out, without asking permission, to pick a narcissus in the garden; or, if he felt that his foot had been imprisoned too long, he would take off his sock and wriggle his toes about, as if it were the most natural thing in the world. The teacher often found drawings in his exercise books, and nearly always the same ones —small red rectangles and microscopic people, equally red.

"And these, what are they meant to be?" the blonde young woman asked him one day.

As if it wasn't obvious!

"Gasoline pumps, miss."

"Why do you draw them all the time?"

Porphyras got up from his seat, his dark eyes glowing with enthusiasm.

"Miss, we had a garage in Epirus, on the road to Janina, the big Patagos Service Station. I was in charge of the gasoline pumps—I served foreigners who were on their way to Athens to see the Parthenon. I had a red uniform, as red . . . red as . . . as . . ."

His eyes swept the classroom.

"The sort of red you don't have in Holland, and Mina and my mother and everyone thought I looked very fine."

The teacher smiled and left him to his drawings, sure that he would soon grow tired of them. But she was wrong. In spite of all his troubles, and the gray skies of Holland, Porphyras had lost nothing of his normal zest. The dream he had cherished for so long had not died. Nearly every afternoon, as they came out of school, and Mina set off home with Johanna, Porphyras would say to Piet: "Shall we go?" He did not have to finish: Piet knew what he meant. Pedaling like mad, they shot off along the straight road, raised like a dike and edged with meadows, that led to a village called Kruinen, with not many more houses than Simitra before the earthquake. But how could they be compared? There was not a single muck heap to be seen at Kruinen, not a chicken or a duck in the streets, no black

64

pigs like those you always saw at Simitra, and no grapes or figs drying on the terraces. Only houses so neat they looked as if they had been put there the day before, each one wearing a bouquet of flowers in the buttonhole of its white-painted windows. Right in the middle of the village, there was a single garage. It was a modest little place, with nothing ostentatious about it. There were not many cars on the Goederen peninsula (that Porphyras had taken for an island on his arrival), since most stock breeders preferred horses to motors. The garage undertook repairs mainly for agricultural machines and tractors. There was no dazzling scarlet gasoline pump as at Janina, only a small hand pump, and quite often the drums were simply emptied straight into the tanks.

In spite of this slight drawback, Porphyras could not resist dragging his friend Piet to Kruinen nearly every evening, though it must be said that Piet was not altogether unwilling. Porphyras always talked about all the things he was interested in with such enthusiasm that he would have converted stones.

The owner of the garage, much amused at the way the young Greek's eyes missed nothing, gave them the freedom of his workshop.

"Porrrphyrras!" he would call out, rolling the "r's" terrifically. "Clean up these grease spots for me, will you?"

Porphyras would grab a rag and start rubbing away. In Holland, people who know how to polish properly are very highly esteemed, and Porphyras soon won the respect of his "boss," as he called him. Soon he was allowed to blow up a tire, or tighten a nut, in addition to his normal job of cleaning up patches of grease and oil. He was even called upon to handle gasoline. Emptying cans into a tractor was obviously nothing like filling up an expensive car; but the smell of the gasoline was almost the same, only not quite so strong as in Greece, where the sun gives strength to colors and smells.

65

Above all, Porphyras felt completely at home in the garage, so much so that he thought: "The matron at Timiza was right, I'm nearly grown up now. Selling gas is great fun, but I ought to know something about mechanics as well."

Whenever his "boss" was repairing an engine, he hung around, and insisted on wiping up every drop of oil that fell, so that he could watch every move.

One day a peasant from the Goederen water meadow brought in an enormous tractor. It was towed in by a horse, since the engine would not go. Every time an attempt was made to get it on the road again, the engine coughed, snorted, trembled, sniffed, hiccuped, and finally stopped with a prolonged sigh. Porphyras and Piet gave their whole attention to the examination of the motor. But the proprietor, in spite of all his skill and experience, could not find the reason for this abnormal behavior on the part of a machine that was nearly new. Whatever he tried, the engine snorted, hiccuped, trembled, and passed out with the same sigh.

The next day the tractor was still there, in front of the door. The proprietor, on the other hand, seemed to be absent.

"You're an expert, Porphyras," said Piet, meaning it. "You know what's wrong, don't you?"

Porphyras had not the slightest idea; but he felt that it would be in extremely poor taste for the son of a former garage owner to admit his ignorance.

"That's where the trouble is," he said, pointing to the engine, and shrugging his shoulders.

"You think so?"

"Practically certain."

He had not pointed at anything specifically, and his "practically certain" did not sound very convincing. Piet, however, was tremendously impressed with his knowledge.

"Well, then, since you know, why don't you try . . ."

Blood rushed to Porphyras' head. Piet had just said the forbidden word. With one bound, Porphyras leaped upon the enormous machine like someone climbing to the attack, and settled himself in the seat. He could now look down upon Piet from a height of more than six feet. The least he could do, now that he was up there, was to cast a knowledgeable eye over all the incredible array of tubes, gears, levers, and knobs.

"That's where the trouble is," he said for the second time; and because he felt he must be more precise, he pulled down one of the levers with all his strength.

Piet only just had time to throw himself out of the path of the juggernaut. Without warning, the tractor took off, with a succession of bangs and jerks like the back-kick of a zebra startled by cannon shot. Porphyras was nearly thrown from his seat, but managed by some miracle to hang on. So there he was, lumbering off into the streets of Kruinen on the back of his monster machine, leaving behind him a flabbergasted Piet choking in a cloud of smoke.

"Ah! *Lieve Hemel!*" What a ride! Terrified, Porphyras could only try to steer a straight course and avoid running anyone over. As it was, he knocked the vicar's bicycle down as it stood beside the curb, and squashed a basket of vegetables left behind by the frightened grocer. Icy sweat was running down his face. At last he came out on the long, straight highway, where he could make some effort to stop his mount. What a hope! He put his foot down on a pedal that could easily have been a brake, and the tractor raced along even faster. Turning the wheel this way and that, he just managed to keep on the road. What if he met a herd of cattle? And what was this small village drawing near? It was his own! He would be going past his own door! . . . And after that? Yes, that was the point. He reviewed the position rapidly. Let's see—going out of the village a road turned right; it would bring him back again. There you are; the circuit's all worked out. He started on his crazy circular tour: twice, three times, he went through the village.

"Porphyras! Porphyras!"

That was Mina calling, but he had no time to wave.

Another turn to the right, and he was on his fourth lap.

Again he tried, moving the first lever that came to hand; but the tractor was determined to pay no attention. Poor Porphyrus began thinking of the dike, and how it led straight to the sea. This infernal machine would be forced to stop in the water, and he could just throw himself into the sea. No; a captain must either save his ship or die on board. But he could not keep going around in circles. It was dusk, and soon his path would be filled with cattle returning home. Well, there was nothing else to do, so off he set for Kruinen again. Turning the wheel so abruptly that he nearly flung himself into the canal, he got into a straight line once more. This time, it was as though the tractor sensed the garage, as a horse senses its stable. Porphyras, only a moment ago red in the face with all his exertions, now grew pale. He had a feeling that he was coming into danger. Here was the bridge over the lock . . . the windmill . . . the big farm . . . the village was drawing rapidly nearer: it was there. The tractor, overheated by this long escapade, seemed to have wings. It swooped down upon the main street, regardless of passers-by; they must get out of the way as best they could.

Calamity! At the far end of the marketplace a herd of cows came into view. Ten, twenty, thirty cows. Porphyras gave himself up for lost. He was faced with terrible alternatives: either he must plunge straight into the herd and massacre the poor beasts, or dash himself to pieces against a wall with his machine.

He had shut his eyes tight to avoid seeing what happened, when his mount suddenly bucked, coughed, snorted, and stopped, having run out of fuel about a yard from a terrified cow. The villagers came running, crowding around the young boy; and among them he saw his "boss." Within seconds Porphyras had recovered his normal composure.

"I was only trying it out," he said. "I knew the trouble

70

was in the . . . in the . . . it's going fine now—it's a very good tractor. . . . Well, I must be off now."

With never a backward look, he went off with his friend Piet, who would never know if Porphyras really did have a special knowledge of mechanics, or how much he had suffered on that nightmare ride.

10

"Dearest Porphyras and Marina,

"Today I'm no longer writing from Lyssira. Two weeks ago I left the Home at Thessaly, and returned to Epirus with my sister, who had at last been released from the hospital. When I left Timiza, it was winter. Now I come to it again under the hot summer sun. Grasshoppers chirp among the cypresses and the cedars, but I must confess the poor town is very downhearted. They're only just beginning to rebuild the houses. It will be years before everything is all right again.

"We're living in a wooden hut. At night it's so hot inside that we prefer to sleep out of doors. A new school has just been opened, and that's in a hut too. Half my old friends will never be coming back. I miss them . . . and I miss you too, my dear Porphyras. I shall never forget our beds side by side in the big dormitory at Lyssira, and the way you held out your hand to me in the night when I was so unhappy.

"Just now the first currants are ripening, and the green figs as well. I wish I could send some to Mina and you too. But

*you are so far away. So I'll just put a little sprig of rosemary
in my letter. I picked it yesterday on the road that leads to
Simitra, and I thought of you. It comes with all affection
from your friend*

Zaïmis."

Mina handed the letter back to Porphyras, but kept the
sprig of rosemary. She shut her eyes and breathed in its scent.

"It's like being suddenly back home again. Do you remember, Porphyras, those great tufts of rosemary that grew along
the bank at the top of the cedar slope? Do you think Zaïmis
picked it there?"

"Maybe."

They were sitting on the wooden bench outside the
stables. Mina looked up at the sky, at a small strip of blue
almost immediately swallowed up by gray clouds.

"Oh!" sighed Mina. "Can it possibly be summer? It's July
now, and nearly as cold as when we came. There's hardly
any more sun. Perhaps there's no summer in Holland!"

"Yes there is, Mina . . . but it's not the same. Look at all
the flowers at the windows, and in the gardens. There
weren't any as beautiful as these in Greece."

"But they smelled nicer."

Porphyras forced a smile.

"Oh, girls! They only think of scent!"

Mina ignored his little joke. Porphyras realized that his
sister was near to tears. If only Zaïmis had not written! . . .
His letters aroused too many memories.

The children sat silently together. Then Mina said, "You're
heartless, Porphyras; you're already forgetting Simitra, our
home there, and all we've lost. You'd be happy anywhere, so
long as there were gas pumps and garages!"

Porphyras was cut to the quick, as he had been when
Zaïmis reproved him for his zest for living.

"You know quite well, Mina, how much I wish you were
happier here. What's the point of being in Greece now? Mrs.

73

van Hoolen treats us just like her own children, and we've lots of nice friends at school."

"And of course there are the cars and the tractors!"

"You're being unkind, Mina. If you remember, you used to be proud of my red uniform. And you know that if it would make you happy, I would forget all about cars and garages."

She made no reply, for she was unwilling to confess that she had tried to hurt him; but she took her brother's hand and kissed it.

Days passed. Summer never came. As far as the two young Greeks were concerned, it was not summer when it rained every other day and no one could ever take off his woolen clothes.

One evening when the van Hoolen family were having their supper in the big kitchen, a room as glossy and polished as one in a museum, there came a knocking at the front door. It was a stranger. He wanted permission to camp in the newly mowed field behind the farm with his car and trailer.

He did not speak in Dutch, but in another very different language, softer sounding, and one that all Dutch children learn at school, together with their own.

"A Frenchman!" exclaimed Porphyras when the stranger had gone.

"Yes, a Frenchman," said Mr. van Hoolen approvingly. "We see plenty of them during the summer, all through the holidays. Very pleasant people."

"Very pleasant," repeated Mrs. van Hoolen. "Though it's a pity they let their cigarette ash drop off just anywhere, and forget to wipe their feet when they come in."

Next morning, as soon as he was up, Porphyras, attracted by the car, went to prowl about behind the farm, and without much difficulty came upon the campers. A long and beautiful white trailer was drawn up in the shelter of a hedge. Porphyras examined it on all sides for a long time, until he saw the stranger of the previous night coming out of his house on wheels in search of water.

"Good morning!" Porphyras said in French. He had been studying the language very diligently at school, and was glad of the opportunity to try out his knowledge in conversation.

"Good morning!" The stranger greeted him with a smile.

Porphyras offered to go to the spring for him. And that was how they became friends. Next day Porphyras and Mina were invited into the trailer.

"Oh!" the little girl exclaimed. "It's just like a real house!"

She knew only a few words of French, but in spite of that handicap made friends at once with Anne-Marie, a little girl of her own age.

"Anne-Marie . . . Marina," she said. "They're almost the same." The two girls did in fact look rather alike, with their olive skins and dark hair.

Porphyras and Mina were astonished when the stranger began talking to them in their own tongue, or rather in the language spoken in Greece when there were temples standing with towering pillars and marble statues.

"It's quite simple," said the stranger, in response to the silent but eager question in Porphyras' eyes. "In France we learn Greek at school—ancient Greek."

"Why?" asked Porphyras.

"Because your language is an ancestor of ours."

Porphyras smiled, at once very proud and amused to discover that he was, in a way, the ancestor of a man very much older than himself.

After this, Porphyras and Mina, and Johanna and Piet as well, were invited to the trailer every evening, after the French family had returned from exploring the surrounding countryside by car. They would all crowd in together, Mina always next to Anne-Marie. The mother made tea on a tiny stove, and then they all drank it and ate cookies.

75

More often than not, Piet and Johanna never said a word, while Porphyras, and then Mina, bombarded the others with questions. Their curiosity was aroused by France, so vast beside Greece or Holland.

"Is it warmer than here? Do olives and grapes and oranges grow there as they do in Greece!" Mina would ask.

"Some regions are like Holland . . . and others like Greece."

"So you do have olives and vines and orange trees?"

"Of course."

"And rosemary and wild thyme as well?"

"We do."

Mina thought she must be dreaming. Then she looked at Anne-Marie, whose skin was so different from Johanna's, and she thought, "It really is true!"

It was certain that one day Porphyras, in spite of the bitter comments of his sister, would be driven to ask certain vital questions. Were there lots of cars in France? What were the filling stations like?

"There are a great number of cars in the town we live in," said the Frenchman. "And the garages look like beautiful sparkling white houses. You see, we're on the busiest road in France, the one that goes down to the south, to Marseilles, the great Mediterranean port . . . which was built by your ancestors, by the way."

"I know," said Porphyras, with an approving nod. "I've seen the name on a map." And he added, "Do they have gas pumps in these garages?"

"Of course, and plenty of them, there are so many cars on the road."

"Ah!" sighed Porphyras.

These foreigners enjoyed talking. They liked telling about their travels, and kept records of them in several albums.

"Have you been to Greece as well?" Mina asked.

"We've been to Athens, Corfu, Salonika, Larissa, Arta . . ."

76

"Arta!" said Mina. "That's near where we lived. Did you think our sky very beautiful too?"

"I don't think we've seen such clear and glowing skies anywhere else we've traveled."

Mina was delighted. For a moment she was able to forget the unceasing gray shadows of the Goederen coast.

But one day, when Mina and Anne-Marie were sitting side by side looking at photographs together, the mother came and put her arm around their shoulders.

"Make the most of it—it's your last evening together. To-morrow we'll be gone."

"Be gone," repeated Mina. "You're—you're going away?"

She had forgotten that the trailer had wheels, and could travel along roads.

"We've been here ten days now, and we want to visit Belgium before we return to France."

"So soon . . . I believed . . . I thought you would be staying for always," Mina said, turning to the little French girl.

Next morning, the car and the trailer had gone. Mina sat down on the flattened grass and stayed there, brooding. For ten days she had forgotten about the Dutch sky. Now the clouds seemed to have come lower, so low that they hung upon the rooftops.

"Porphyras, I wish I could have gone with them. If only they'd sent us to France, I wouldn't have been so miserable."

Porphyras shook his head.

"I think you're unhappy because we've no home of our own and no one belonging to us any more. So it would be the same wherever we were."

"It wouldn't!" she assured him. "It wouldn't be the same. You don't understand, you're only a boy. Boys don't understand these things. All you think of are your garages and your engines. You wouldn't even worry if you lost me!"

"Oh, Mina, you're saying that just to hurt me, you're

77

being unkind like you were the other day. Why do you say things like that?"

"For fun!"

She ran off, and Porphyras had a hard time catching up with her. When he did, she flung herself, weeping, into his arms. What could he do but forgive her?

11

"*Come and see!* All the fields have gone, and the trees and the houses! There's nothing left!"

"Your eyes must not be open yet, Mina!"

"Not a thing! Even the dike has disappeared. It's terrifying!"

Porphyras got up and joined his sister at the window. Mina was not dreaming; the trees, the houses, the dike had all gone. Terror stricken, Mina was clinging to her brother's arm when a voice called from the courtyard below:

"Now then, up there, why are you sticking your noses in the air? It's not the right sort of day to go looking for airplanes!"

Mina was reassured to hear Piet's voice.

"What's happened, Piet? We can't see a thing!"

"*Lieve Hemel!* Haven't you ever been in a fog before?"

They never had. Fog was as unknown in Greece as the turpentine tree in Holland. They went down into the courtyard.

"It's like this in September every year," Piet explained. "It

79

means that summer is over, and autumn storms are not far off."

"Summer over? But there hasn't been any summer." Mina sighed.

They had to light the lamps on their bikes to go to school that morning. It was impossible to see five yards ahead along the dike. Cars crawled along, their yellow eyes only just piercing the thick fog.

"Do they last a long time, these fogs?" Mina asked anxiously.

"It all depends. Sometimes it's only a few hours, but most often we have it for quite a few days. Last year it stayed over a week. The wind blows it away . . . and I can tell you it's not a warm wind!"

"Not a warm wind," Mina repeated, pulling her raincoat down over her knees.

Piet knew what he was talking about. In the evening of the second day the wind came to shake the big poplars along the canal, scattering clouds of dead leaves, and the fog was dispersed. It was autumn now.

"If only the answer to our letter would come before winter!" Mina said.

"You mustn't be impatient, Mina."

"Do you think they'll let us go back?"

Porphyras did not know what to say. Two weeks earlier, without saying anything to Mrs. van Hoolen, he had given in to Mina's entreaties and written to Greece asking for permission to return to their own land. Since he could not complain of illness or ill-treatment, he didn't have very much hope.

"Those of our friends who stayed behind," he said, "are very much worse off than we are."

"So *you* think!" said the little girl, who did not believe him.

When the letter did arrive, it was a bitter disappointment. They were told that they ought to be ashamed of complaining, that they would never be happier than they were at the moment, and that the first return party was not planned to take place before the following summer. Porphyras found it almost impossible to console his sister.

"Don't cry so, Mina dearest! The winter will go by quickly. Think of those big logs Mrs. van Hoolen kept burning when we first came here. . . . And we can skate when the canal freezes."

The day following the arrival of the letter was a Wednesday, always a free half-day for Dutch schoolchildren. After a week of stinging gales, the wind from the sea had calmed down. It was warm, with long spells of sunshine, and the sky was almost clear.

"Let's go for a good long walk together, shall we?" suggested Porphyras.

Mina shook her head.

"I'm sick of going to the garage to look at cars and tractors with their insides out."

"We'll go the other way, as far as the Kruinen water meadow."

She shook her head again.

"What about Gravelinen, then—the market town? Or anywhere you like."

"I'd rather stay with Johanna on the farm."

He sat beside her on the bench outside the stables. She did not speak; she was trying not to seem sad. Normally, Porphyras was never to be found on the farm on Wednesday afternoons. He began to think of the garage at Kruinen; his "boss" was expecting, any day now, the delivery of the doctor's new car from a German factory. Porphyras was dying to see it, but he had no intention of running off without Mina if she wanted to be with him.

"Are you quite sure you don't want to come for a walk, Mina?"

"I promised Johanna I'd help her to make Piet's birthday cake. . . . But you go, it's such a lovely day."

He did not quite like to go. He was ready to give up all

81

thought of the Kruinen garage and take her wherever she would like to go, if only she would smile.

"Here is Johanna," she said. "She's bought the flour. You can go now."

Porphyras hugged her and ran off to find Piet. By unspoken consent, they made for Kruinen. A few people, curious to have a look at the doctor's new car, which had just that minute been delivered, were assembled in front of the garage. The two boys inspected all the glittering chromium and nickel plate. Porphyras pictured himself in his red uniform: that car was just about worthy of such glory. Then almost at once Mina's bitter smile flashed through his mind when she accused him of being only interested in cars. All his pleasure left him. He walked around the wonderful car a few more times, and said:

"Shall we go?"

Piet could not believe his ears. Porphyras had never before suggested that it was time to go.

"Don't you like it?"

"Of course I do, Piet. Only, you see, mechanics like us— well, we're only interested in breakdowns . . . It won't be long before we'll be seeing it at close quarters."

"That's so," said Piet, who had every respect for his friend's skill.

Although Porphyras was in such a hurry now to get back, he had to go into the village first with Piet, who had shopping to do. Then, delaying him further, when they were halfway across the dike on their way home, he had to stop and mend a puncture in his back tire. It was difficult to repair his bike in the gale that was blowing again. Piet had never seen the Greek boy so clumsy with his hands. When at last they reached the farm, it was growing dark.

"Where's Mina?" Porphyras asked at once.

"I don't know," said Mrs. van Hoolen tranquilly. "I haven't seen her for quite a while. . . . But it's not late yet."

He went out into the yard again, and saw Johanna coming

out of the dairy, carrying a bowl of cream.

"Where's Mina? She told me she was staying in with you this afternoon."

"She helped me make the birthday cake. Then she went off for a walk."

"Which way?"

"She said something about Gravelinen . . . she'll soon be back. What are you looking so worried about? You don't think the wind will carry her off, do you?"

He made no reply. Clearly, no one on the farm was anxious about her; he alone was afraid that something had happened to her. However, he just waited, without saying anything.

"It's certainly getting dark," Mrs. van Hoolen finally said. "It's not the first time Mina's gone off for a walk by herself, but she's never come back so late before."

Porphyras questioned Johanna again.

"That's all I know," the little girl answered. "It was about half-past three when she went off, just after we'd put the cake in the oven. I saw her walking along toward Gravelinen. She waved to me."

Another half-hour went by. By this time the whole family was anxious.

"It's rather strange," said Mr. Van Hoolen, looking at the clock hanging on the wall. "We'd better go and see what's happened. Porphyras, get your coat and come with me."

Outside, in the dark night, the wind tossed dead leaves into swirling drifts as it grew wilder. The man and the boy walked along side by side. Porphyras was silent, asking himself questions over and over again. If Mina had only gone for a walk, she would be back by now. Something had happened to her. But what? That letter from Greece was at the bottom of it all. Mina had not been the same since it arrived.

They reached Gravelinen and went into several shops to make inquiries. No one had seen the Greek girl. At last, however, they found a baker's boy who thought he had seen her going along the dike that crossed the big water meadow.

"About what time?" Mr. van Hoolen asked him.

"It was still daylight . . . she looked as though she was in a hurry."

"You're certain it was her?"

"You can't mistake her. No one else around here has such an olive skin and dark hair."

Mr. van Hoolen turned to Porphyras with a questioning look.

"I don't know what she's up to," the boy said. "She told me nothing."

They battled along the dike, a steep embankment about a mile and a half long, that led straight to the coast. At every step Porphyras thought he heard cries for help. But it was only the wind. Breathless, they came to the end of the dike, which lay buried in sand. The sea was invisible, yet made its presence felt, angry and menacing. The only house upon the shore was the customs man's hut, which had a light showing in its tiny window.

"Do go in," begged Porphyras, trembling with cold and anxiety.

An elderly customs man was dozing in a chair, his arms along the back, his legs outstretched at each side of a miniature porcelain stove gently purring with heat. The old man started, rubbed his eyes, and listened.

"That's right, a little gypsy."

"No, not a gypsy," corrected Mr. van Hoolen, "a little Greek girl. But certainly dark enough to . . ."

"That's what I meant . . . yes, I saw her; I asked her what she was doing all alone on the shore. I must have scared her; she ran off at once, in that direction."

"Did you see her come back?"

"No, I didn't. Though, with night coming on . . ."

"And you haven't heard any cry for help?"

"Don't be funny. With this wind you couldn't hear the siren on the ferry boat from Shouven, even if it was only a quarter of a mile away!"

Hardly daring to breathe, Porphyras hung upon every word. Why had Mina come to that desolate windswept shore only to get lost? Why, oh why?

"Mr. van Hoolen, we've just got to help her. She's fallen down on the shore, she's waiting—listen! She's calling me! She's calling me!"

But it was only the wind, and the screaming gulls.

"If you like," said the customs man, "I'll go over this shore a little later . . . though I'd be astonished if . . ."

"Oh no, sir, not later, at once! She's calling us!"

The good man lit his lantern, a strong lamp that no hurricane could put out; but it shed such a small glow in the vast darkness. The sand, still wet from high tide, was difficult to walk on. They breasted the wind, the customs man walking in the middle between Porphyras and Mr. van

85

Hoolen. From time to time he raised his lamp so as to throw light upon some piece of flotsam ahead. Each time, Porphyras' heart stopped beating. Where are you, Mina? Oh, where are you?

They plodded on for a long time, until the customs man came to a halt.

"Believe me, if she's lost her way along here, she won't have stayed on the shore to get frozen. You'll find her asleep in some shelter somewhere tomorrow morning . . . or even at home by the time you get back."

That was what Porphyras was secretly hoping. Retracing their steps, they came back to the hut. The customs man offered them a mug of tea to refresh them, after which Mr. van Hoolen and the boy went off toward the farm.

"I'll find her back home, back home," Porphyras went on saying to himself, to keep up his courage.

Midnight sounded as they were going through the sleeping town of Gravelinen. Nearly two miles to go. Porphyras was dropping with fatigue.

"I'll find her back home, back home."

At last they saw the farmhouse, or rather the lighted rectangles of two windows. Porphyras summoned enough strength to run. The tall silhouette of the Dutchwoman was framed in the lighted doorway.

"Mrs. van Hoolen!" he cried breathlessly. "Is she back? Is she back?"

12

Mina had not come back. Next morning, they all tried to believe that, as the customs man had suggested, she had spent the night in some makeshift shelter and would return of her own accord. But that hope soon left them. Anxiety grew into anguish. Porphyras, beyond tears, was completely overwhelmed.

Mrs. van Hoolen stayed with him the whole morning. While the farmer, who had harnessed his best horse, went to Kruinen to inform the burgomaster of the child's disappearance, and to give the police all details, his wife did what she could to get to the bottom of the mystery.

"Are you quite sure, Porphyras, that she told you nothing?"

"Nothing."

"Yet you seemed so worried yesterday when you and Piet came back from Kruinen. I didn't pay much attention at the time; but I do remember that you asked me where Mina was the minute you got in the house . . . and Piet tells me you were anxious to leave the garage much earlier than usual."

"I know, I was a bit worried."

"You know you can speak quite freely to me, Porphyras. Did anyone on the farm do anything to upset her badly? People are sometimes clumsy even when they don't mean to be!"

"Oh no, Mrs. van Hoolen, Mina loved you all, you've all been so good to her."

"Well, then?"

"I just don't know."

"Could it be anything to do with that letter you had from Greece?"

Porphyras hung his head and his face grew red. There was a silence.

"Yes, perhaps," he said.

For a moment he hesitated. Then he realized that even if it hurt Mrs. van Hoolen, he must tell her what had happened. He explained how unhappy Mina had been since her arrival in Holland, because she could not get used to a country so different from her own. She was afraid of the coming winter. So one day he had written to the orphanage at home. Oh no, he'd said nothing against Mr. and Mrs. van Hoolen, simply that Mina was unhappy and the Dutch sky always sad. The answer had been a terrible shock to Mina. "And that's all," said Porphyras. "That's all I know. . . . But please don't think that she was unhappy because of you. . . . And I'm sure she didn't mean to run away!"

He looked up. Mrs. van Hoolen was crying.

"Poor children!" she murmured, taking Porphyras' hands in her own. "I understand only too well. Nothing can ever take the place of our own country, our own home. Don't try to apologize . . . I feel we should apologize to you, because we don't always know how to help you to forget your grief. I did so hope that this house would become your own. Still, what you tell me gives me a gleam of hope . . . Mina will come back. Where could she go, what would become of her, without you? The poor little thing!"

Porphyras allowed himself to feel hopeful again. The burgomaster of Kruinen had put an announcement about the disappearance of the little Greek girl in all the regional newspapers of Goederen, in case anyone should come upon her.

Two days later, in the early afternoon, a stranger appeared on a bicycle and knocked at the farmhouse door. Porphyras went pale when he recognized the long green oilskins worn by the fishermen of Zeeland. Oh, God! Had his sister's body been washed up by the sea?

"I've come about that little refugee you had here," the stranger was explaining to Mr. van Hoolen. "I saw the notice in the paper. I didn't want to disturb you for nothing . . . but at the same time I thought . . ."

"Tell me quickly!"

"Well, I don't know anything much, really, except that the night the little girl disappeared my small *shaerboot* went too."

Porphyras shivered.

"Where do you come from?" Mr. van Hoolen asked.

"From Zeegen, three miles away."

"From Zeegen! Mina could never have covered such a distance by night . . . and what would she be doing with a *shaerboot*?"

The man shrugged his shoulders.

"Exactly. That's just what I said to myself. But I thought I'd better let you know, because of the coincidence. My boat didn't untie itself from the dike."

Mr. van Hoolen thanked the fisherman for the trouble he had taken, and asked him into the kitchen for a cup of coffee.

"Well now, Porphyras," the farmer said, as soon as the stranger had gone off on his bicycle. "What do you think about that?"

Porphyras had seen plenty of *shaerboots,* small flat-bottomed boats that fishing boats towed along when the sea was not too rough.

"Mina was terrified of water," he said, "especially the sea. She would never have dared to get into such a small boat all by herself, at night . . . But she does sometimes do unexpected things."

The following day he went off to see for himself the tiny port of Zeegen, hollowed out of the massive sides of a dune. He found the fisherman without any difficulty, and the man showed him the exact spot where his *shaerboot* had been anchored.

"That night," the man told him, "the sea was as wicked as a dog when you snatch his bone away. The bravest girl in all Zeeland wouldn't have dared face it . . . and you say your sister was scared of water. Why, then, *Lieve Hemel*, should she take my boat?"

Porphyras returned to the farm very downcast. Days went by, bringing no trace of Mina. Every morning Mr. van Hoolen harnessed his mare and went to the *stadhuis*, the town hall, in case the coast guard had recovered a body.

The whole farm was sad and silent. Porphyras hardly slept or ate. His eyes were enormous in his thin face. At night he told himself endlessly, "It's all my fault. I shouldn't have left her that day—just because of the doctor's car. I wanted to see it too badly. I loathe cars! I hate garages! If I still had my tunic and my cap, I'd tear them to pieces and trample on them!"

As the best way of punishing himself, he tore up all the pictures of cars he had so lovingly cut out of newspapers and pinned up on his bedroom wall. Every morning he went to meet the mailman, in case Mina should write. The rest of the time he searched the house from attic to cellar, believing that she must have left word somewhere.

No one from Simitra would have recognized Porphyras, the Porphyras who found life good and believed in luck. Now shadows made him tremble. If at dusk a seagull, borne by the wind, uttered its harsh scream over the house, he would tear out in a frenzy, because he thought he had heard his sister calling for help. And everyone on the farm tried to soften his grief, to help him go on hoping, even though no one believed any longer that Mina would come back.

"You know you can take my word," said fat, good-hearted Piet. "Everyone knows I never tell lies. . . . Well, then, I tell you the sea never waits so long to give up its dead. Cross my heart, Mina didn't mean to run away, and she hasn't fallen into the sea! I *know* she'll come back, Porphyras!"

"She will come back! She will come back!" Those were the only words he heard. Porphyras, too, went on saying them . . . but not aloud. He was afraid of lying . . . of deceiving himself.

A week passed, another, and yet another. Each day brought winter one step nearer. In Holland, winter is never terrible, only damp and gray. Porphyras had no interest in anything, not even in school: he went there only to kill time. Not once had Piet been able to persuade him to visit Kruinen.

"No, Piet, I'll never stop in front of a garage again, never!"

He spent his free half-day scribbling Greek words on paper torn from his exercise books, and going off alone on his bicycle, pedaling furiously against the wind.

"I'm afraid he's going a little crazy," Piet told his mother one day. "I followed him, without letting him catch sight of me. He's carrying bits of paper around, and he puts them in the field, on the shore, all over the place, with stones on them to stop them from being blown away. . . ."

But Porphyras was not at all mad. If Piet had known any Greek, he would have read, "Dear little sister, come back quickly." Or "Mina, forgive me." Or elsewhere, "I promise never to think of cars again." And if Piet had been able to look into his friend's mind, he would have realized Porphyras knew that Mina would never find those papers. It was simply a way of taking the edge off his unhappiness.

The day came, however, when his grief was unendurable. Porphyras genuinely saw no reason to go on living. Whether he returned to Greece without Mina, or stayed in Holland, life had no meaning.

More and more frequently, he wandered along the canal. Its waters were so calm, so serene, so happy. It had no thoughts, and nothing it contained, its grass or its pebbles, was burdened with thinking. One day he approached the very edge and sat down on the sodden grass.

"The water doesn't move; it seems to be asleep. I wish I could sleep again."

Then he leaned over: his heavy head fell forward. A passer-by, strolling along the bank just then, wondered what the boy was looking at so intently on the surface of the water. Porphyras was not looking at anything; he was waiting for his feverish brain to be at peace.

He had to wait a long time. Suddenly there was a slight noise in the water. Plop! The placid surface wrinkled into widening circles. A frog had just hopped into it. A frog! All at once Porphyras saw Papa Christophore in his mind's eye, heard him laughing and saying, "Red attracts frogs, not cars!" It was the day they had discussed his red overalls. Memories crowded in upon him: his mother, Simitra, the shining skies of Greece. Lovely memories are a wonderful treasure house. . . . Was it really true that there was no more happiness for him?

Suddenly his desolate eyes saw in the water, or rather in the sky reflected in it, a little patch as blue as the Greek sky. Porphyras was back in his own land, and it seemed to him that the warm wind of Thessaly was touching the nape of his neck. Could it be? He came back to the present. A cow was watching him, waiting patiently for him to move so that she could come down to the canal to drink. He knew her well; she was called Moseete. Mina had once tried to milk Moseete, and the cow had slapped her across the face with her tail. A little smile flickered across his face. Moseete was a good beast; he began to scratch gently between her horns, and she seemed to like it.

"Tell me, Moseete, do you remember Mina? Animals know things that human beings don't. Mina isn't dead, is she? Tell me she isn't dead!"

Moseete looked at him as if she had understood the question, and slowly swung her great head from left to right. She had certainly said "No." Mina was not dead. Porphyras cradled her big head in his arms and kissed her between the horns, saying:

"Mina! Mina! You're not dead."

He set off for home, tearing across the fields like someone who had just discovered a long-lost treasure.

13

"*You can believe it* or not, as you like, Porphyras, but I've just seen a truck as high as a house and as wide as that; fantastic!"

"Where?"

"At Kruinen. It's come from Osterberg, a terrific truck— twenty-five tons! You'll never guess where it's going. . . ."

"How d'you expect me to?"

"There was a big F on the rear number plate."

"A French truck!" Porphyras exclaimed.

"Yes, a French one, and going direct to Paris. It was loaded with seed potatoes, and stopped at the service station for minor repairs. It will be back again."

A French truck. For weeks now Porphyras had been thinking of that vast unknown country. France, the land of agreeable travelers living in trailers, the land where Mina would have been less unhappy . . . where maybe she was to be found. If his sister were alive, it was in a country like France, that reminded them of their own, a country where olives and rosemary grew.

"A French truck?" said Porphyras. "And you say it will pass this way again?" His deep sigh betrayed his longing.

It was December now. Johanna had torn fifty pages from the calendar in the kitchen since the day Mina disappeared. As far as everyone knew, Porphyras had thrown off his terrible grief and was much the same as he had always been. He joined in the games of the other children, went back to the garage at Kruinen, and took fresh pleasure in cutting out more cars from the newspapers to pin up by his bed. But appearances were deceptive. Porphyras had forgotten nothing. If Mina were not dead, he must go and look for her.

That evening he could think of nothing but the French truck that had traveled across the Goederen peninsula. An idea was growing in his mind, one that did not need the Greek sun to bring it quickly to maturity.

Every day as he came out of school, he pedaled along in the deepening night to Kruinen, to find out when this marvelous truck would pass through the village again. No one took much notice of these heavy transports, since they were familiar sights in the region.

At last, one afternoon the garage owner said to him: "What a pity, Porphyras! If you'd been here half an hour ago, you would have seen that famous truck you've been plaguing me about!"

Porphyras felt his cheeks grow pale.

"It's gone?"

"It went straight through to Osterberg, to pick up a load."

The boy breathed again.

"So I'll be able to see it on the return journey?"

"Indeed you won't! It's scheduled to pass through late this evening or tonight. Heavy trucks like that are just like trains—on the road in all weathers, and all hours of the day and night."

Porphyras asked no more questions. He puttered about in the garage a little longer, wiping up patches of grease here and there, after which he got on his bicycle and returned to the farm.

All through supper he was preoccupied and hardly said a word. Fortunately, Piet had not gone with him to the garage, so there was no risk of his mentioning the truck, since he did not know that it would be passing through.

"You're not very talkative tonight," Mrs. van Hoolen remarked. Porphyras put aside his problems and began to tell them how he had seen a new type of tractor at Kruinen (which was true), a much more practical proposition than a certain one that had taken him for a ride over the meadows.

When the meal was finished, he kissed in turn and according to ritual, Mrs. van Hoolen, Johanna and Piet, shook hands with Mr. van Hoolen, and went up to his room.

He was going, yes, he was going, but it would be a wrench. He had been in Holland for almost a year, and found it a welcoming country in spite of its gloomy skies. At the farm, he had been taken into the family, been a brother to Johanna and Piet. To leave was to suffer, to lose a new family, and to hurt others as well. Mrs. van Hoolen had wept bitterly when Mina disappeared. Of course, it wouldn't be the same sort of thing as far as he was concerned. He would write. In fact, he would write now, so that they would not be anxious about him.

He tore a page from his school exercise book, and was reminded that he was also going to lose thirty blond young friends with whom he had been happy. But the page was torn out, and ready. He wrote:

"My dear Piet,

"I am going away: I am very sorry. But I must go. Mina is alive; I must find her. I don't know whether I will ever come back. I hope your parents will forgive me. They don't deserve this new trouble; they have always been so good to both of us. Tell them not to worry; I will write to you. My dear Piet, I give you all my love, and kiss Johanna for me. I will never forget you.

Porphyras."

He undressed and went to bed, intending to get up again as soon as everyone was asleep. He knew it would not be long, for no one kept late hours on the farm. He waited half an hour; then, not hearing a sound anywhere, he got up and stuffed a few things into the small suitcase that was exactly the color of the Dutch meadows. Mrs. van Hoolen had bought it for Mina the day of the parish fair at Kruinen. He read over what he had written earlier, unable to stop thinking of the pain he was bringing to the van Hoolens; and he added at the bottom of the page, "Tell Johanna to scratch Moseete between her horns. Mina loved to do that."

His bedroom was on the first floor, and not very high up. Thick turf grew outside even in winter. There was no danger of being heard or seen if he were to jump, for the rest of the bedrooms faced the other way. He leaped into space, and landed unhurt on the wet grass. As he got up, he found that he was still reluctant. He knew quite well that it was wrong to leave like this. He and Mina had been sent to Holland because everyone thought they would be happy there; he was only a child, and had no right to take matters into his own hands. But what else could he do? Would they have understood? Mr. and Mrs. van Hoolen were not his parents, and could not take full responsibility for him . . . and he just had to take this opportunity at once. As soon as he reached France, he would write to his own country, so that the authorities could see it was not just a silly escapade.

He walked over the long dike, carrying his small green case. He had not even had to think up a plan; this one had come ready-made into his head. He was setting off amid sea breezes toward a new future and unknown territory, but his heart was untroubled. He was thirteen, he would find Mina, he had all his life before him.

As he went through deserted Kruinen, he glanced in passing at "his" service station, where so many treasures were at rest behind the closed doors. The village was behind him now. He thought of Mina. She, too, had walked on into the night . . . where had she been going?

He walked on and on. The small case he carried made his arm ache, and he began to grow anxious. The truck might have gone by already. Eleven strokes of a clock were brought to him on the wind. He came to a halt. He must have time to get back to the farm before dawn, if his plan came to nothing. Half an hour went by. At last in the silence he heard a heavy rumbling. It was the truck; he knew it at once by the driving lights on each side. Without any hesitation, he planted himself in the middle of the road, until the blinding arcs of the headlights came down on him like a fusillade. Then he waved his arm, without putting the case down, and went back to the side of the road to wait.

The truck came on quickly, in spite of its colossal weight. Porphyras wondered whether the driver had seen him. He went back and stood in the middle of the road, quite forgetting how a similar episode, on a certain road in Greece, had nearly ended tragically. The night was rent by the prolonged screeching of the truck braking and groaning to a standstill only a few paces from him. Two immense silhouettes tumbled out of the vehicle: one of them came up to the boy, and, taking him by the collar, shook him like a rat.

"Are you crazy, standing in the middle of the road like that? You might've been squashed as flat as a pancake—or thrown us into the ditch!"

The driver exploded in French, but Porphyras understood every word. For some time now he had been making wonderful progress in the language.

"Monsieur, I didn't realize . . . I . . . I just had to . . ."

"That's no reason for getting yourself crushed to a pulp! Where are you heading for?"

"I don't know—I mean, if you want me to explain, let me go along with you, and I'll show you the place."

"All right, then, hop in quickly."

The man got hold of Porphyras as if he were a loaf of bread and heaved him with his case into the cab, a cab so

98

huge and so wide that it could easily have taken four people. There was a revving-up of the engine, a clashing of gears, a turn of the wheel, and the truck was off. Porphyras felt lost between the two giants. Were all Frenchmen so wide at the shoulder? The one in the trailer had given the impression of being rather slight. He tried to make himself small, very small, as he hugged his case close to him.

"You don't seem to realize, lad," the driver went on grumbling, "that a truck like this can't pull up like a scooter!"

"I'm sorry," said Porphyras, who had not understood the word "scooter."

"And where d'you want to be put down?"

"Farther on—a few more miles—I'll show you."

Porphyras would have been happy to spend the night in that well-warmed cab, in spite of the surly tone of the two men. But that was impossible. They would soon reach the frontier post, and what would these Frenchmen think if he admitted that he had no idea where he was going, and that no one was expecting him? They would say, "So you don't know? You just want to leave home? Oh no, not so fast!" and they would put him down in the road. No, he must go through with his plan to the very end. When they had gone five or six miles, he pointed to the outlines of a sleeping house set back a little from the road, and just showing in the darkness.

"There it is."

Brakes screeched; the truck slowed down. Porphyras thanked the men warmly.

"Good night, *Messieurs*," he said in French, taking care to pronounce the words correctly.

"*Goede ewond*," the two men replied, hoping to please the young Dutch boy.

Porphyras slipped down from the cab and got out of the range of the headlights as soon as he could, but made no attempt to reach the isolated house. In the darkness, he began to run behind the long truck, which had already started off again. He threw his case onto the sacks of potatoes, so as to free his hands. Then, finding a stanchion to give him a grip, he heaved himself aboard. Ouf! Just in time! The inside of the truck seemed huge. As if the sun of Greece were still warming his brain, he thought it as vast as the church at Simitra. How was he to find a place among these sacks? They were so closely packed it was impossible to slip a hand between them. Fortunately, right at the back the last row was incomplete. He made a little nest for himself, then a sort of corridor, so that he could stretch out. He smiled after all the excitement and the exhaustion. It was just as well that he had not climbed in here at once, when he had forced the truck to pull up. The drivers would have been suspicious: they might even have checked their load. Whereas now he could safely sleep as soundly as he liked.

Sleep, yes, Porphyras wanted nothing better. His head pillowed on a sack of potatoes, he was deeply asleep before the wheels of the truck had revolved a hundred times.

When he awoke, dawn was breaking—a reluctant dawn, gray and unwashed. His back was sore; it felt as bruised as if he had slept on a heap of pebbles. It was not the coming of dawn that had snatched him from sleep, but a potato jerked out of a sack by a too sudden halt and descending upon his nose. How long had he been sleeping? Where was he now? He heard the cab door open. The sound of footsteps and voices drew near, and seemed to be coming toward the back of the truck. He shook in his shoes when a hand pulled back the canvas flap at the back so that light from outside filtered in.

"Have you only these two hundred and thirty sacks to declare?"

"That's all."

"Drive on."

Of course, the frontier . . . but which one? They had spoken in French, so this must be France. He must have crossed the other frontier during the night, without his knowing it.

France! It was odd, but he felt he had somehow drawn nearer to Mina. How far away Holland was now! This was the time the farm came to life; they would discover that he was missing. "Mrs. van Hoolen, please forgive me!" he thought.

He grew colder in spite of the raincoat wrapped tightly around him. It grew lighter, and he wanted to know what this new country looked like. All he could see was the road streaming away from him between two rows of sentinels. Without such sentinels, all the roads in the world would be exactly alike. In this case they were tall, leafless poplars like those of Zeeland. Was France like Holland, then? . . . If it was, they'd lied to him when they had talked about olive trees and even orange trees! The truck drove on, crossing mighty plains, traveling through towns that showed him only their pointed gray slate roofs, and small villages smelling of dung heaps. Paris, the town they said was so big and so beautiful, seemed a long way off. He would have been more patient if only his stomach had not begun to torment him cruelly.

Then the truck slowed down and came to a halt. The two drivers got down. Porphyras could hear something being unscrewed. Of course, they were getting the tank filled. In spite of all his good resolutions, Porphyras succumbed to his consuming interest in garages. Were gasoline pumps the same in France? He crawled between the sacks, lifted his head up like a snake, unbuckled one of the leather thongs that held the flap in place, and carefully lifted the thick canvas. Oh wondrous sight! A dozen pumps stood in a row in front of a long and very new building, wonderful shining automatic gasoline pumps standing to attention, hose on shoulder. And the last splendid touch was that the man in charge of them, like the one at Janina, wore a uniform. Maybe it was not a glowing red tunic; but the blue overalls, adorned with a crest also to be found on the cap, were nevertheless elegant. And there was more than one uniform. Porphyras suddenly became aware of two other mechanics in the same get-up.

As he was watching, one of them came forward to serve a motorist who had just drawn up at the pump next to the last. Porphyras lifted the canvas flap a bit more, then higher still, and craned his neck . . .

A sudden oath made him jump. Turning his head, he saw a threatening finger pointing toward him. Too late for concealment, Porphyras! The gasoline pumps have just played a dirty trick on you.

"You little devil! So that's why you made us pull up in the middle of the night, is it? Just for a lark!"

With no mercy for the potatoes he was trampling over in his heavy boots, one of the two men, the bigger one, plucked the boy from his hiding place, pushed him roughly along, and forced him to get down into the road, where he stood shaking with fear and cold and hunger.

"I am so sorry!"

"A fat lot of good that'll do you, you little rascal! You've had a good run for your money, and now you're going to pay for it!"

"Oh, please, mister, please listen—I didn't want—I——"

"That's enough!"

Then turning to the manager of the service station, he said:

"Where's the nearest police station? . . . on the way to Paris?"

"It's at Verviers, about fifteen miles away."

The police! Porphyras understood the word, and it made him afraid. When he was a very little boy, someone in Simitra had told him about a man who was hanged for stealing a basketful of melons from a field.

"I'm not a thief! I'm not! I'm not . . . I haven't taken a thing, I only wanted to find my sister, my sister Marina. . . ."

"You can explain all that to the police. Now get up in the cab with us!"

103

And the truck set off again, leaving behind the imposing service station with its mechanics in uniform; while Porphyras, between his two bodyguards, gave way to tears.

14

Who would ever have believed that that surly truck driver, once he had heard Porphyras' story, would not only fail to hand him over to the police, but would take him under his own roof, even though he already had five children of his own to feed? Porphyras smiled as he remembered his initial fear of the man, and then got up quietly because of little Raymond, who slept in the same bed.

"Up already!" said Madame Bruneau. "You get up too early!"

"I must get going. Perhaps I'll be luckier today."

Madame Bruneau gave a little nod as she went on peeling potatoes.

"Whatever you do, Porphyras, wrap yourself up well. It's freezing this morning. Look!"

She put down her knife and held back the curtain at the window. Porphyras looked out. As far as the eye could travel, a sea of roofs stretched beneath a gray and woolly sky; and today that sea was white.

"It snowed in the night, and this morning it froze. Winter's really here. It's a dreary season, winter!"

"Drearier than in Greece," Porphyras answered. "If Mina were here, she'd be downhearted. She loved sunshine so much!"

Madame Bruneau said nothing to this. To stop him thinking on those unhappy lines, she began to pour out his coffee.

"Oh, that's enough! That's enough!"

"You must have more, Porphyras, while it's so cold. It helps to warm you up. How many slices of bread shall I cut?"

"Two, please."

"You had three or even four the first few days. Don't you like this bread? . . . or are you feeling ill?"

"Oh no," said Porphyras, making an effort to smile. "I'm not ill. Is there any shopping I can do, since I've got to go out?"

"Get the bread, as usual . . . and you might look at the new grocer's, the one on the corner. They might have cheaper vegetables."

She persuaded him to put on an extra sweater made from an old one of her own, for her children were younger than Porphyras, and then he slipped on his raincoat.

"And whatever you do, don't play the same trick you did yesterday!" said Madame Bruneau, her voice gently scolding him. "Come back for your dinner. I was terribly worried; I kept thinking you must have fallen under a bus!"

Porphyras grew red, miserably aware that once again he had caused anxiety. Madame Bruneau kissed him. He went off; but he had only just reached the landing when he turned back and opened the door again.

"Madame Bruneau, I like you so much!"

He would have liked to say still more, but he could think of nothing else. It was too difficult to put his feelings into words. His face reddened again; he smiled to hide his embarrassment. Closing the door, he ran down the seven

106

flights of stairs in the old house, across a small courtyard dark as a cellar, and out into the street. It was certainly very cold: passers-by walked briskly along, with their coat collars turned up and their hands deep in their pockets.

Right? Left? He tossed the only coin he had left to see whether it came down heads or tails, as he had done every morning so far. It came down tails, so he turned left. His eagerness was dwindling. Paris was too big a city, and the sun was too often missing. Had Mina come and lost herself here? He wandered along slowly, instead of walking at a good pace to warm himself up, as all those who passed him were doing.

"I've already been in Paris twelve days," he murmured. "Twelve days."

He recalled the cramped two-roomed apartment he had just left. "No," he thought, "I can't stay; they're too poor. People living in two rooms at the top of a house and feeding on potatoes and precious little else every day can't have any money. I mustn't stay, even if Madame Bruneau tries to persuade me."

Once already he had made some feeble excuse for not coming back to eat at midday, so as to save a meal.

"Porphyras," he said aloud. "You're not a beggar. It was different at Kruinen, the farm was wealthy. Here, it would be a terrible thing to do."

He strode along, rubbing his ears because they were stinging with the cold, and went on talking to himself. "Paris is such a big city, you're bound to get work if you look for it."

To start work, to earn his living! It was a brand-new idea. So far, it had simply been childish enjoyment when he had filled a tank with gasoline, or stuck his nose under the hood of a car. Brought into contact again with poor people, forced to consider ways and means, to count every penny, he was reminded of Papa Christophore, of his mother, and his poverty-stricken childhood. To be a year older is tremendous. When you have had the luck to be born under a sky that brings plants and human beings to maturity far earlier than anywhere else, you are a man at thirteen.

He walked the length of the boulevard, and turned into a busy and not very wide street he had never been in before. He was not worried by any fear of getting lost. He had an instinctive and extraordinarily good sense of direction. As it happened, he loathed the subway, that infernal railway in the bowels of the earth, where the tunnels smelled so nasty, and there was nothing to see. He had only traveled on it once, with Madame Bruneau; and when he came up again he was completely lost.

He was walking through a very crowded district, probably one given over to business, and not far from a station, for people carrying brief cases went by. He stopped in front of a big café to admire a waiter in a stiff white shirtfront who brought drinks to the tables with wonderful dexterity, balancing on his fingertips a tray loaded with bottles and glasses. Farther on he stopped again, this time before the window of a photographer's shop. He was not interested in the cameras on display but in the sample photographs fixed on a large screen, most of them pictures filled with sunshine, where happy children played on the golden sands of gleaming beaches. Some of them made him think of his own land, because of their cacti and palm trees and tall fluted columns all shining white.

In one of these photos, a little girl, sitting on stone steps at the foot of an enormous marble jar, was stroking a kitten. He could not see her eyes, but there was something in the shape of the dark head, the thin arms, the way she was bending over to stroke the little creature, that reminded him of Mina. For a long time he stood looking at the little photo. He shrugged his shoulders. Ten times, twenty times, he thought he had come upon his sister in the streets of the great city; ten times, twenty times, he had been mistaken.

He turned his back on the shop and went on, whistling to keep up his courage. Time passed. It was nearly noon.

Women carrying full shopping bags were coming out of the grocers' and the bakers' shops. A little later, he found himself surrounded by men, hurrying along, frozen, to the nearest subway station. Soon the rush had died down. He was walking on without quite knowing where his feet were taking him when he came to a sudden halt on the edge of the pavement. A signboard on the other side of the street had caught his eye and held him prisoner. Twice, three times he read:

CHEZ XAROPOULOS
THE ACROPOLIS RESTAURANT

Xaropoulos! A Greek name, there could be no doubt about that! And *The Acropolis Restaurant!* Could there be any other Acropolis but the one at Athens? Apart from the signboard, the restaurant was like any other in the street. Several shadows moved behind its curtains; the restaurant was open.

When his excitement had died down a little, he ventured to cross the road and try to peer into the restaurant. Suddenly the smell of frying with olive oil assailed his nostrils as it arose from the basement, almost at his feet. He leaned forward. The delicious smells, so long forgotten, were coming from a grating level with the pavement. He bent down to look into this black hole, but he could see nothing, only hear voices. Were they speaking Greek?

Bent double, he tried to overhear them, as he went on sniffing at the rich appetizing smells. A very uncomfortable position! He sat down, his back against the wall, as near as possible to that sweet-smelling hole.

He had been enjoying for quite a time the mingled smells of oil, onion, and saffron, that made him very conscious of his ravenous hunger, when a hand touched him lightly on the shoulder.

"Get up now and go away! The boss doesn't like beggars around the door!"

Porphyras came out of his dream. He jumped, and raised his head to the man who had spoken to him.

"Come on, quickly now!" said the waiter impatiently, flapping a napkin as though he were swatting flies. "Be off with you!"

He seized Porphyras by the sleeve and dragged him to his feet. The boy stared intently at the man, whose black hair was carefully oiled and brushed back, and who had a swarthy skin and narrow eyes.

"I'm not a beggar," he said. "I haven't asked for anything."

Without thinking, he had spoken in Greek. Before he had finished his sentence the waiter's face had changed.

"Well, I'll be darned! You're Greek, a young Greek boy! What are you doing here all alone? Are you lost?"

Porphyras shook his head, and tears came into his eyes, though he would not let them fall.

"No, I'm not lost . . . I was just passing . . ."

He began to walk away along the street, with every intention of leaving the area; but hunger, cold, and excitement made him stumble. The waiter caught up with him.

"I can see you're hungry. . . . Wait a bit, I'm going . . ."

Just then the proprietor came out, furious with the waiter, who had let himself be buttonholed by this ragamuffin when he was in the middle of serving customers.

"Don't send him away, sir, he's Greek."

The great Xaropoulos pursed up his lips. Porphyras explained how he had left Greece after the great earthquake.

"You're on your own in Paris?"

"Well—I'm staying with Monsieur Bruneau."

"Which Bruneau?"

"Very nice people."

"I suppose you're hungry? . . . or you wouldn't have come sniffing around . . ."

Turning to the waiter he said, "I can't bother with him now, Alkis. Take him to the kitchen and tell them to feed

110

him."

Porphyras went along a corridor, and was taken down a narrow spiral staircase to the basement. A chef in a white cap and two women with their sleeves rolled up were busy at a long kitchen range. The heat was suffocating, heavy with the smell of hot oil and herbs. The two women were not at all pleased at having this intruder thrust upon them in the rush hour.

"Sit here," said one of them, clearing a corner of the table.

Porphyras went meekly, stupefied by the heat and his emotion. The woman put down in front of him an enormous plateful of rice prepared in Greek fashion, highly spiced and filled with black olives. The boy hardly dared begin on it. These people were not Greeks, and they obviously resented his presence. As soon as he had finished eating, they would throw him out as if he were a starving dog, to be pitied one moment and chased off the next. But the olives smelled so good, it was such a savory rice! He could not resist it. When his plate was licked clean of the very last grain of rice, he stared at the big saucepan with such longing eyes that the cook, still muttering under her breath, gave him a second helping.

"Ah, Mina! If only you were here, you could close your eyes and believe you were back in Simitra."

When his meal had ended with a handful of figs and raisins, he was filled with an indefinable sense of well-being, much as he felt in the past when, after a meal, he would stretch out in the shade of a cedar or a fig tree, and give himself up to wonderful dreams as he dozed off.

Was it the enormous meal, or the suffocating heat of the kitchen? Whatever the cause, his head lolled over on his shoulder, and he fell asleep, deaf to the clatter of plates, the voices, the shouted orders. He was back in Epirus, by the side of the road leading to Arta, the sun was burning his skin, and soon he would set out with his goats for the mountain slopes; he would stare into the sky to discover the first

111

stars. Mina, close beside him, was also basking in the sun.
. . . But what did she want? Why was she shaking him by
the shoulder?

He started up, his eyelids flickering. It was not Mina, it
was the waiter who was shaking him. Embarrassed, he did
his best to excuse himself.

"That's the first time I've ever dropped off to sleep like
that!"

The waiter grinned, and explained that upstairs the restaurant was now closed.

"The boss wants to see you . . . he seems to think you're
looking for a job."

"He's right," said Porphyras. "I am."

They went upstairs into the restaurant. Xaropoulos was
busy with his accounts behind a small counter.

"Ah, there you are!" he said, looking up.

The two enormous dishes of Greek food had made a new
boy of Porphyras, for the proprietor added:

"By all the Gods of Olympus, what a difference! . . . Is
my kitchen responsible for this miracle?"

"I don't think I've ever had a feast like it in my life!
It made me think I was back in our own land."

Then, as he looked around the room, he saw huge painted
panels showing familiar scenes—the Acropolis, the road to
Salonika, the Bay of Arta.

"In fact, I *am* back in Greece."

"Yes, they're good, aren't they?" Xaropoulos said.

"They are indeed!" Porphyras approved with all his heart,
quite dazzled by their beauty.

Then the proprietor began to question the boy, asking
him where he had come from and why he had left.

"Ran away? You ran away?"

"No, not really. I'm trying to find my sister Mina."

"And you expect to find her in Paris?"

"I'm sure she's in France . . . I wish I could work here,
sir."

114

"Here?"

"Oh, yes!"

"You think I can take you on just like that?"

"I'm certain they'd leave me with you, sir, since you're Greek."

The proprietor sighed.

"You're very young; it's unwise for me to . . . Oh well, we'll try to get matters put on a proper footing. . . . I don't like to leave a young compatriot to starve. Let's see, I'll write to Greece right away, and meanwhile you can consider yourself under my protection. Have you ever done any dishwashing?"

"Dishwashing?"

"In other words, can you wash up? It's a hard job."

"That doesn't matter."

"You can help the waiter, Alkis, too, in the rush hour. We've a good number of Greeks settled in Paris among our customers. They enjoy coming here to speak our own tongue, and order their meals in Greek. So you can give Alkis a hand."

The proprietor scratched his chin.

"Now, as for your wages, I shan't be able to offer you a seat in Olympus, as we say back home. Business isn't too good at the moment, and it's not as if I really needed you. But you'll get your food and some tips. Will that do?"

Porphyras agreed that it would. He was so happy he was ready to kneel and kiss the feet of this Greek with the flabby face and the cunning look of a jackal. He was so eager to show his gratitude that he offered to go down to the kitchen at once and help wash up.

When he left the Acropolis, he found that it was still cold outside, but a quite bearable cold that stung the face only to make the mind more alert. He went by the photographer's shop on his way home. Mina was still there, stroking her kitten. He looked at her for a long time. Tears came into his eyes. Where was she now? He felt ashamed of that sumptuous meal, much too good for him, and the wonderful smells with which his clothes were still impregnated.

"Mina," he whispered. "Just stop stroking that kitten for a minute. Look at me, tell me where you are. Are you wandering about this big city? I only hope you are as lucky as I am just now. I'll come and see you every day in this shop, and one day perhaps . . ."

He set off happily, ran the length of the boulevard and bounded up the seven flights of stairs in the decrepit apartment house.

"Madame Bruneau! I've just found my own country again! —I've got a job! I'm going to earn some money! . . . Oh! Paris is the most wonderful city in the whole world!"

15

It was almost as cold as it had been in the depth of winter. Occasionally snowflakes drifted from the leaden sky and a vicious little wind blew them into your face. Porphyras hurried along at a fast pace, wearing his raincoat as always.

"All things considered, I shouldn't be complaining. It's warm in the kitchen at the Acropolis, and I certainly eat well."

He was trying to put a good face on things; but it was an effort, and he knew it. Since he was early, he thought he might as well go the long way around before he went in.

"There's no point in being early," he thought. "It won't make Xaropoulos any sweeter, and he'll only find more work for me to do."

He took another road, not so busy as the one near the Acropolis, and quite unknown to him; and there he came upon a garage. A car was drawn up by the curb because of engine trouble. A pair of legs protruded from underneath the chassis. He stopped, looked closely at the car, and bent down to see if he could discover the owner of the legs. They belonged to a youngster who, wrench in hand, was tightening a nut . . . or rather, trying to tighten it; for it was certain by the way he was swearing, just like a grown man, that the nut was not co-operating.

Very much interested, Porphyras crouched still lower. The young apprentice suddenly became aware of this unknown head watching his lack of skill, and his bad temper was unleashed upon the spectator.

"What d'you think you're doing?"

"Nothing," smiled Porphyras. "Only looking."

"Just looking and trying to get a rise out of me, eh?"

The nut rolled into the gutter as the apprentice, wriggling from underneath the car like an eel from a mudhole, came and stood in front of Porphyras.

"So you want to know what I'm up to, do you? Well, I'm just getting warmed up to give you a clout!"

With the back of his hand he landed a well-aimed blow, and Porphyras, quick as Jove's thunderbolt, returned the compliment. It had all happened so quickly that both boys were astonished at the speed of their reactions. They stood face to face, speechless, not knowing what to do next.

"There's no need to get mad at me," Porphyras said, bearing no malice. "I wasn't jeering—I might even have lent you a hand."

"Honest?"

"I know a bit about cars; I used to work in a garage."

"Why didn't you say so, then?"

"Well, you didn't exactly give me time!"

They began to laugh like a couple of kids who have just played a good trick on each other.

"It's this blasted nut I can't get into place. It needs to be held while I turn the bolt. I'm on my own here just now."

"Let's see."

They both slid under the car. The bolt was in fact in a bad position, but, by working together, they managed to screw

118

on the nut without too much trouble.

"There you are!" said Porphyras. "Nothing to it!"

But when he got up, he saw that his fine Dutch raincoat was covered with oil stains.

"It's not as bad as it looks," declared the apprentice. "We can get it off with gasoline. Come over here."

They went into the garage, where the atmosphere was filled with a delicious blending of grease, oil, gasoline, and rubber. As well as he could, Porphyras cleaned his raincoat, adorned as it was with magnificent rainbow patches. The two boys began to talk together as though they were already fully qualified mechanics.

Not for long; for Porphyras caught sight of the moonface of a clock in the office attached to the garage.

"I must get a move on, I'll be late."

"Where d'you work?"

Porphyras hesitated.

"In a restaurant."

"Oh, a restaurant!" the other replied, with a somewhat scornful expression on his face. "I suppose it's cleaner than a garage, but I wouldn't want that sort of job."

His comment stung Porphyras, who pretended that he had not heard it. The two boys shook hands warmly, and Porphyras hastily set off. As he walked along he was thinking:

"He's right, it's a cleaner job, but it's not the job for me. I couldn't make out why I've been so miserable these last few days, but I know now. I'd rather smell a garage than a kitchen, even one full of saffron and paprika and thyme and pepper. Perhaps if I really had found my own country again at Xaropoulos' restaurant . . . But he gives me so little freedom, only two hours a day from three to five."

When he pushed open the door of the restaurant, the proprietor, standing with his hands in his pockets, looked as though he was lying in wait for him.

"Well, Porphyras," he said, glancing at the clock at the

119

far end of the room. "Twenty past five! . . . And what d'you think you look like? Have you seen yourself in a mirror? . . . I do believe you've been fighting, you've got finger-marks all over your face! Be sure it's the first time and the last! Is that clear?"

Porphyras nodded, walked past the proprietor and went down into the kitchen to cut bread, fill salt cellars and the oil and vinegar bottles, before going to help Alkis, the waiter, to set the tables.

He had been living at the Acropolis for about a month now, in a room under the rafters, a very small room hardly lighted at all by a tiny circular skylight. At a moment's notice, he had taken the place of one of the kitchen hands, a girl whom Xaropoulos had sent packing at once.

It must be said that Alkis had taken the trouble to warn him, when he left the Bruneaus to settle in at the Acropolis.

"You're making a mistake, Porphyras. You don't know Xaropoulos yet. He loves money. As soon as you're in his clutches, he'll take advantage and exploit you as much as he can."

The boy had not listened. He did not wish to be a burden on the Bruneaus any longer, even though they wanted to keep him with them. But Alkis was right. Porphyras slaved now from morning to night, on the grounds that he was given board, lodging, and laundry, and that he was only a child. It would have been bearable if only he could have found himself at home again among the Greek customers. But how could he find Greece again among people so different from his parents and friends in Simitra or Lyssira?

"The ones that come to this restaurant are all wealthy people," Alkis had told him. "Of course they enjoy meeting each other here, and speaking their own tongue, but that's all there is to it. They've grown rich in Paris; Greece only reminds them of when they were poor."

"Oh, Alkis, do you really think they wouldn't be glad to see our own lovely sky again?"

"Yes, but only in passing, while on a cruise. They're not true Greeks any more."

In his kitchen, where the sun never penetrated, illuminated day and night by neon strip-lighting that had a strange effect upon faces, Porphyras began cutting bread with the special machine fixed to one end of the table. But he was not giving his mind to the job. He could not forget the young mechanic's delight in his work. As so often before, his imagination carried him off to service stations, gasoline pumps, bright red uniforms, and the one the dressmaker at Simitra had made for him.

"Do you remember, Mina, how well it suited me? You were so proud of your brother then. I wonder if you'd recognize him today, trapped in this cellar like a small, frightened mouse? But he hasn't lost heart, you know. At bottom, he's still the same Porphyras, the one who climbed trees to fetch pomegranates for you, and found life wonderful!"

Suddenly a cry rang out. The chef dropped his ladle and spun around. Lost in thought, Porphyras had not noticed the difference between his finger and the bread. Blood was streaming from him. The kitchen maid, in hysterics, went up to fetch the boss, who strode in in a very bad temper. The chef had meanwhile wound a clean rag around the wounded finger.

"I don't know what happened," Porphyras said apologetically. "The bread must have slipped."

"I'm not surprised," growled Xaropoulos. "I'd just like to know what you were up to this afternoon! Don't you forget, young man, that you're in *my* charge now. . . . You ought to be ashamed of yourself."

"I didn't do it on purpose," murmured Porphyras. "I don't know what you mean."

Blood was still seeping through the rag. The boy had to be taken to the doctor, who found it difficult to stop the bleeding, and finally put two stitches in the finger.

"Of course," said Xaropoulos, still grumbling. "It would

121

happen just as we're about to open!"

He looked at the big dressing, that made Porphyras' finger ten times its normal size.

"How can I send you in to help Alkis with a thing like that?"

Porphyras hung his head. Was it really his fault? What could he say to Xaropoulos, who never stopped grumbling at him for one reason or another? That evening, he only went into the restaurant to clear the tables, when the place was shut. Since he could do no washing up, Alkis did it for him. The waiter was a kindly man, and had taken Porphyras under his wing. If only Alkis were the boss!

That night, in his folding bed, the boy could not help shedding a few tears, though he quickly pulled himself together again.

"Porphyras," he told himself, "don't be such a baby; you're thirteen now, remember. Go to sleep. Tomorrow you won't be feeling so downhearted and you'll be able to get a grip on yourself again."

For a long time shooting pains in his damaged finger kept him from sleep, and the dressing added to his discomfort by being too tight.

"Mustn't give Xaropoulos another chance to bawl me out," he was telling himself as he at last fell asleep.

The next morning he got up before the time fixed by the proprietor. He had decided that since his finger in its cocoon of bandages slowed down all his work, he would begin the day's labors earlier. Xaropoulos would see from this that he was not unwilling to work.

He came into the deserted kitchen, dark as a cellar, switched on the light, and fetched some potatoes, peeling them as well as he could, with the bandage always in the way. He had not been there more than five minutes when he heard footsteps coming down the stairs. From the bottom step the hairy Xaropoulos, his eyes swollen with sleep, glared at him suspiciously.

"What are you doing here at this time of day?"

"I'm just peeling potatoes, to get an early start on my work, because of my finger."

Xaropoulos could find no answer to that. He folded his arms and came into the kitchen. He at once noticed that the door of a cupboard containing kitchen cloths and also canned food, among them jars of olives, was half open.

"Why is that door open?"

"I needed a cloth to wipe the table, because it was greasy —look, here it is."

The proprietor looked at the cloth, and then went to close the door, muttering something unintelligible under his breath. Then, turning abruptly to Porphyras, he said:

"It's easy to see *you* don't pay the electric light bills here. Lighting up just for you. . . . You never think. . . . To-morrow, be good enough to get up at the right time; and if you can't get through your work you can just take time off your two free hours. . . . That'll teach you to pay more attention in future!"

This was so unfair that Porphyras began to feel rebellious. He had gotten up so early only to get started on his work, and he was being treated like a spendthrift, if not a thief!

He was heavy-hearted all day long. He spoke to no one but Alkis.

"Business isn't so good just now," the latter explained. "That's why he's so bad-tempered."

Porphyras gave up his two hours of liberty for a whole week. He felt as though he were living perpetually in an oven: it was horrible. But at last the doctor took off the bandages that had hampered him so much and he regained his former speed and dexterity in his work.

How wonderful it was to breathe the fresh air outside once more, to see the sky again, and imagine he was free. As he crossed the threshold he stood still on the pavement and drew in a deep breath of city air. The sky seemed radiant to him, though in fact it was heavy with gray clouds. It seemed to him that he could dismiss Xaropoulos' flabby face and bullying voice from his mind forever. His first thought was for Mina. He went straight to the photographer's shop. Mina was still waiting there for him, stroking her kitten. He began to talk to her:

"Mina, I know now you're not in this great city. Just tell me, dearest, where I should look for you . . . Tell me, Mina, answer me!"

He pressed his head against the window, waiting, and suddenly he could imagine her saying:

"Porphyras, don't waste your life looking for me. I don't know whether perhaps we shall find each other again some day. But don't count on luck too much. Do what you ought to do. Remember our home at Simitra, and the things you dreamed of then. And forgive me, Porphyras, for having upset you sometimes, in Holland, when I was so unhappy."

He stared at the little photo for a long time, smiled at it, and went off almost lighthearted. For a long time he wandered through the streets. The Acropolis seemed a long way off, as though it belonged to the distant past, now gone beyond recall. He felt as if his two brief hours of liberty would last forever.

The illusion did not last very long. The precious minutes flew by as fast as dead leaves in a winter's gale. It was already time to be on his way back. All the same, his footsteps flagged, and it seemed as though something were holding him back. . . . He suddenly wanted to see the young garage hand again, the one he had met the other day. The garage was open. He strolled past several times, hoping for a glimpse of the boy's blue overalls. He must be away on some errand. Porphyras moved on, stopped, turned, and came back once more. As he was passing the garage again, he saw a man glance at his watch. He shivered, and ran after the stranger, to ask him the time.

"Just five, my boy."

He began to run, had to stop to tie up his shoelace, and

arrived at the restaurant out of breath. As once before, Xaropoulos looked across at the chiming clock.

"I'm sorry I'm five minutes late," Porphyras said quickly. "I ran as hard as I could. I haven't been out for a week, and it was so good . . ."

He had obviously said the wrong thing. He had no means of knowing that only a few moments earlier Xaropoulos had come upon a discrepancy in his accounts.

"Good!" roared the boss. "The young gentleman comes back late because it was good to be out, and has the nerve to tell me so, grinning all over his face, as if that was all that mattered!"

Porphyras tried to protest.

"I'm only five minutes late, I can make them up in no time."

Xaropoulos, beside himself with rage, went over to the boy and boxed his ears.

"I'll teach you lost time can never be made up, you impudent little rat!"

Porphyras clenched his fists. This blow was very different from the almost friendly one given by the young mechanic. This one wounded him—not physically, but in his pride. He gritted his teeth, said nothing, and walked through the room as though he were going to the kitchen. But on the landing he paused, and then, instead of going down, he went up the stairs that led to his attic. Calm now, he packed his things in Mina's little green case. When he came to the threshold of the restaurant again, he was pale and trembling.

"What's all this?" shouted the proprietor, pointing at the suitcase. "What d'you think you're doing?"

In a low but unfaltering voice, Porphyras said, "I'm leaving."

"What? But . . . why, you're joking . . . you're not clearing out because of a miserable slap in the face not worth bothering about!"

125

Holding his case with both hands, Porphyras just stood there, his eyes fixed on the painting of the Bay of Arta.

"Now be sensible," blustered Xaropoulos. "First of all, where can you go? You've no family. . . . You can't have forgotten that you were starving when I took you in. . . . Surely you haven't got any grudge against me?"

His voice grew persuasive. Porphyras stayed where he was. Xaropoulos tried to take the case from him, but the boy's hands closed on it like a vice.

"Come now, Porphyras, be reasonable, you can't mean to leave me in the lurch like this? You need me, and for my part I need you. . . . I'm sorry I lost my temper just now. Forget it, and let's be friends."

The cunning Greek was honey sweet. Though he fought against it, Porphyras found himself relenting. He knew quite well, however, that Xaropoulos had no affection for him, and only kept him out of self-interest. Moreover, so as to avoid possible difficulties, the man had never put matters on a proper footing with the Greek orphanage.

"After all, Porphyras"—Xaropoulos played his part well, putting a friendly hand on the boy's shoulder—"after all, we're both Greeks, and compatriots shouldn't quarrel with each other. Be a good boy now, take your case to your room, and hurry back to help Alkis. What would he do without you?"

He was clever enough to know how to use the friendship between his two employees for his own ends. Porphyras gave a deep sigh. He turned back, walked slowly through the restaurant, and began to climb the stairs. There was a glass door giving on to the yard about four steps up, and today it was half open. Porphyras put his case down and opened the door wide. It was growing dark in the streets. Lights cut across each other. A heavy truck went by, decked out with multicolored lamps like a ship on the high seas. He thought of the truck that had brought him from Holland, of the driver whose voice was not the unctuous voice

126

of Xaropoulos. He thought of all the trucks traveling along the roads of France and all over the world, free as the birds that fly in the air. Just then he heard the proprietor's harsh voice venting his anger on the kitchen maid.

His mind was made up. He picked up his case, walked across the courtyard, and found himself in the street. He crossed over without any special haste, and when he was on the opposite pavement, he turned around. The signboard had just lighted up:

CHEZ XAROPOULOS
THE ACROPOLIS RESTAURANT

He had not in fact found his own country again behind the façade of that house. He went away from it, carrying his small green case with both hands. He would have liked to see the young mechanic again as he went by, but the garage was already closed, since it was Saturday. He trudged along the endless streets. There were chiming clocks like the one in the restaurant shining from the plate-glass window of a clockmaker, and they all showed the same hour.

"Seven o'clock," he thought. "Alkis is setting the tables at this very moment, putting out the little vases of flowers, the salt cellars, the toothpicks."

He sighed.

"I should have said good-bye to Alkis. He'll think I'm angry with him as well."

The crowd in the streets thinned out as he went on walking; but the restaurants were jammed to the bursting point with people. His stomach discreetly reminded him that it was time to eat, but he ignored the message.

His case grew heavier; he kept changing it from one hand to the other. Soon iron shutters were rattling down over shopwindows with a noise like thunder; signboards were no longer visible. What time was it? He felt lonely . . . but he was not altogether alone. He had friends in this great city.

Without really being aware of the fact, he stopped walking aimlessly and began to look at street names. He turned right, then left, down a long boulevard, now almost deserted. Suddenly he stopped on the edge of the pavement and looked up, not quite to the sky, but nearly. On the seventh floor of a tall old apartment house, two small rectangles of light were still shining. His heart thudded.

"They're not in bed yet," he said to himself.

He flung himself up the stairs, and was reunited with his good friends Monsieur and Madame Bruneau.

16

"Did you hear that, Toine?"

"Let me get some sleep, Miette."

"It was a terrific noise—like an explosion."

"You're always hearing extraordinary noises! I want to sleep, I'm tired!"

"I tell you, Toine, something's happened out on the road, near here, over northward."

Toine turned over so that he would not hear his wife any more. Miette Barbidoux knew better than to go on talking, but a few minutes later she slid out of bed as quietly as she could, to see what was going on outside. She had only just reached the window when she cried out. Jolted abruptly from sleep, Toine also got up and joined his wife. In the distance, by the roadside, a gigantic red-hot fire was sending flames as tall as plane trees into the night sky. Toine let fall an oath.

"There's been an accident, Miette. We'd better go quickly and see what can be done."

She threw a coat around her shoulders, while Toine slipped quickly into his overcoat. Outside, the icy wind stung their

129

faces and cut their breath. They ran along the road toward the blaze and heard the crackling of the flames, carried to them on the wind.

"It must be one of those heavy transports, gone up in flames with all its load."

The wind was carrying flame and smoke toward them. They had to make a detour before they could get near. A little farther on, several cars and trucks were drawn up, and their occupants, powerless, were watching the terrible sight. It was easy to imagine how the catastrophe had happened. Such dramas often took place on Highway #7. Sometimes it was a skid; sometimes a driver was blinded by an on-coming car, or fell asleep at the wheel. And then the plane trees, those lovely trees that covered the road with their lacy shade all through the warm summer days, were transformed into menacing giants.

"How awful!" Miette groaned, hanging on her husband's arm. "I only hope the driver got out in time!"

A man looking on reassured her.

"There were two of them. They were able to jump clear, thank God, before the cab went up in flames."

When the fire engine, summoned by a passing motorist, drove up, the load was still being devoured by white-hot flame. Even when the fire was put out, it was a long time before anyone could get near the wreckage.

"Let's go," murmured Miette.

She pulled Toine back. Her teeth were chattering in that bitter wind, and she sighed with relief as she pushed her door open. But they had only just got back when, having seen their light, all the people who had watched the accident that night came trooping into the café, wanting rum, or a hot drink, as treatment for shock. Toine and Miette were kept busy behind the counter, while everyone went on talking about the accident. As Madame Barbidoux closed the door on the last customer, the cuckoo clock in the kitchen announced two o'clock.

It would be a short night. The first transport drivers, who

130

left Marseilles before dawn, would be in very early in the morning for their cup of hot coffee. But Miette was still too obsessed with the sight she had witnessed to be able to sleep. She saw flames everywhere, and could not escape from them. Finally she went down into the kitchen, in case she had forgotten to turn the gas jets off. She had just put her foot on the last stair when she thought she heard someone outside calling for help. She listened. There was certainly someone calling, and from just the other side of the door of the café, the side door near the garage. Terrified, she tore upstairs into the bedroom.

"Toine, someone's calling for help, by the side door."

"Wassermarrer?"

"By the side door, like someone groaning."

"You're sure it's not the wind?"

"Oh no, Toine, it sounds like a woman's voice, or a child's."

Barbidoux got up and went downstairs.

"Listen, Toine!"

Miette had been right. Someone was groaning outside. Barbidoux opened the door. The light fell upon a huddled figure that lifted a face smeared with blood. Miette screamed and recoiled, while Toine leaned forward to get a better view, and saw that it was a boy. He helped him to his feet.

"Poor little soul!" said Miette, recovering from her shock. "You've been hurt!"

The boy looked at her and, seeing her horrified face, found enough strength to murmur:

"It's nothing much, only a cut on my forehead. It's stopped bleeding."

His teeth were chattering. He must have been out for hours in that bitter March night, swept by the icy wind. Toine helped him into the kitchen, that had kept some of its daytime heat. Miette, trembling a little, examined the wound. It looked dreadful because of all the dried blood. But it was, as he had said, only a superficial cut. She washed his blood-spattered face with warm water.

"Why didn't you come straight here, my dear, instead of staying out in the cold? . . . You were in that truck that burned out, weren't you?"

The boy made no reply. His eyes were glazed, and he shook all over.

"He's too cold, too frightened," said Miette. "He can't talk yet."

She heated some coffee and poured it into a big cup. The boy drank it eagerly, but she had to hold the cup for him; it shook too much in his own hands.

"Poor little duck," sighed Miette. "Would you like something to eat as well?"

She buttered a piece of toast, and he nibbled at it, but could not finish it. He tried to smile at Miette to thank her, and she, eager to reassure him, said:

"You're not afraid of us, are you? You're not in a nest of brigands, but in a roadside café. You couldn't have fallen into better hands, could you, now?"

He tried to smile again, but his eyes suddenly grew enormous, with dark shadows beneath them. Toine had only

132

just time to catch him as he collapsed.

"We were silly to try to question him; he's absolutely exhausted. Help me carry him uptairs. Which room shall we put him in, Miette?"

"In the room where the Negus stayed. It's next to ours, and we can leave the door open in case he needs us."

The boy was undressed and put to bed. The warmth of the house had steadied his nerves, but it had also made him drowsy. He was still very pale.

"Should we phone the doctor?" Miette wondered.

"It's very late. We'd better wait until morning."

They stayed by his bedside a while. There was nothing to worry them in his slow, regular breathing, and his pulse was almost normal. Once more, Barbidoux and Miette went back to bed, but this time they did not go off to sleep again.

"It's queer!" said Toine. "I feel he's trying to hide who he is and where he comes from. . . . Somehow I don't think he's French."

"No, you're right, he's got a funny accent; he rolls his 'r's' like a Levantine . . . and I can't make out why he didn't go off with the driver of the truck."

"Don't worry about it, Miette, we'll find out tomorrow. The main thing is that the poor kid's safe."

Next morning, the sun was already high in the sky before Porphyras awoke. And no sooner were his eyes open than he cried out. Framed in the window facing him was a tree covered with blossoms, dazzling white against a sky as blue as the waters of the Ionian Sea. Simitra! He was back in Simitra! His excitement lasted only a few seconds, but it was so intense that it made his heart beat faster. He looked around the room. It was quite unlike his attic at home. His eyes were fixed on the blue striped carpet when he heard the stairs creak. He recognized the two faces that had welcomed him several hours earlier. The woman leaned toward him, asking him if he had slept well, and whether he was in pain.

Porphyras shook his head. She felt his pulse.

"You're not feverish, or at least hardly at all."

"I'm not ill. You mustn't call the doctor, really you mustn't, I . . . I must be on my way!"

"With that pale little face? Not a chance! Where were you going? Who should we get in touch with to say that you are safe and well? . . . You were in that truck that went up in flames, weren't you?"

Porphyras turned his head away, and made no reply. He began trembling again, as he had the night before. A long silence fell upon the room. Toine and Miette looked at each other.

"Look here, you can tell us . . . we won't give away your secrets."

Porphyras looked up at Toine. This man had a good face. Perhaps he was as good as he looked. Toine, aware of the boy's trust, took advantage of it to say:

"What's your name?"

Porphyras still hesitated, but the woman was smiling at him so gently that he said:

"Porphyras . . . Porphyras Patagos. . . . It's a Greek name. I come from Simitra, a village in Epirus."

Then he begged: "Please, sir, you won't tell the police?"

"We won't tell them a thing. Where were you going?"

"I don't know."

"You were in the truck? With the drivers?"

"I was hidden behind, among the boxes. When the truck skidded and crashed into a plane tree, I was thrown from one end to the other, with all the boxes. The truck burst into flames almost at once. I was able to jump down. I ran off and hid in a field. I just stayed there. It was terribly cold."

"Why didn't you come here right away? It was a clear night; you could see the house."

"I was afraid of being locked up and handed over to the police."

"Have you done anything bad?"

Porphyras looked deeply offended.

"No, of course not. I was looking for my sister, my sister Mina."

Madame Barbidoux sat down on the end of the bed. She realized that the boy was still too unnerved to be able to talk freely. He would have to get his confidence back first.

"Are you thirsty? Would you like some goat's milk?"

Porphyras' eyes shone, and his mouth curved into a smile.

"Goat's milk! Oh yes, indeed I would!"

He had not tasted any since he left Greece. As he drank it, he again felt as though he were at home. His eyes went back to the window.

"That tree——" he said. "When I left Paris, all the trees were dead, but that looks like an almond tree in flower."

"It is an almond tree, and the blossoms are just out. Spring is on its way here."

He struggled up to see better, but his head felt dizzy.

"Let him have a bit of rest," said Toine. "Later, when his breakfast has built him up a bit, he might perhaps get up."

Left alone, Porphyras dozed a little, living through last night's tragedy all over again. But the window fascinated him. He got up. As far as the eye could see stretched fields lit by a golden sun, dotted with squat, silvery bushes and tall black flames.

"Olive trees! Cypresses!"

It truly was a countryside like his own. And the little girl over there running after her dog could so easily have been Mina. When Miette Barbidoux came up again to see how he was, she found him quite overwhelmed, with shining eyes. Before she had a chance to ask a single question, he began to tell her about himself, everything there was to know about him. How he had left Paris and the Bruneaus, who had been so good to him, to set out for the big port of Marseilles, where, so he had been told, Greek ships often put in, and where, more important, he had hoped to find Mina again. For it was in that region that those campers in Holland had lived, the ones Mina had liked so much. He did not know their name or their address, he only knew they lived in that part of France.

"Madame—you won't stop me from going to look for my sister, will you?"

"Of course we won't, but you must get really well again first. You're still terribly pale when you get up. Hop back into bed!"

He obeyed her. Gradually the sounds of this isolated house, set on the side of the road, grew familiar. It must be on a main road, for the traffic never stopped. From time to time he heard the screeching of brakes. He suddenly remembered that he had reached a roadside café. With luck, he would be among cars and gasoline pumps too. His old dreams came surging back; nothing could ever destroy them.

When he was able to get up, Toine was only too pleased to show him around the "establishment," for he was very proud of it. Miette was busy in the café, where meals also were served, with foreign tourists wanting hot coffee. At a small table, two truckdrivers, easily recognizable by their broad shoulders and genial faces, were making a meal of bread, sausage, and olives. Two others, farther off, were enjoying a glass of wine and talking about engines. Porphyras was immediately at home in this atmosphere.

"Now come and see the outside," said Toine.

The icy wind was still blowing, almost as strongly as it had in the night. But now it was warmed by a dazzling sun. The air was as crisp as a vine shoot and as light as a firefly; it was a pleasure to be out in it.

"Oh! Just look at all those gas pumps!"

Toine Barbidoux began to laugh.

"What else would I refuel all these cars with? And heaven alone knows how many there are on the road. . . . Have you ever seen anything like it?"

Trucks, coaches, delivery vans, and cars endlessly flashed by and passed each other on this main road edged with plane trees shivering in the wind.

"Highway #7 is the busiest road in France," he added with quiet pride. "It's the road that leads to the sun!"

Porphyras, watching the astonishing sight, forgot the terror of the night.

"There's certainly no lack of work!" Barbidoux went on. "See, here's another customer!"

A car was edging in to draw up in front of the pumps, a foreign car with an English license plate. Porphyras thought it very fine. When the tank was filled, it set off again noiselessly and at great speed.

"As you see," Toine explained. "Some of our customers are really rich. . . . Besides, turn around a minute——"

He pointed to the front of the building. A wide white band ran along the whole face: and on it the Greek boy read in huge gilt letters:

THE EMPEROR'S FILLING STATION

17

"*Dear Zaïmis,*

"*If I tell you that I'm sitting in the shade of an olive tree, and that in the distance I can just about see a mountain, with snow still white upon its summit, showing against the deep blue sky, you will think I'm writing this from Greece, that the olive tree is in Epirus, and the mountain part of the Pindaran chain. However, I'm still in France, and France is such a huge country! The province I'm living in now is so like our own land that sometimes, when I go for a walk, I almost expect to meet you!*

"*But I don't often go for walks, Zaïmis, for I'm working, yes in a garage, or rather in a filling station, on a main road of a kind that doesn't exist in Greece. Do you remember my telling you, in the Home at Lyssira, about my wonderful red uniform? And how you teased me? Well, I've got that uniform, only it's not red but blue, because France is a country where everyone is very fond of blue. The uniform has a crest with a wonderful seashell embroidered on it. And I sell gas all day long. Oh, Zaïmis, if only you could see the*

138

traffic on this road, it's incredible! . . .

"I'm with very nice people. To tell you the truth, I found them one night quite by accident, just like a melon in a field of lentils, as we say back home. I'll tell you about that later. They have no children, or rather, only a daughter who has just married and gone abroad. They treat me just as if I were their own son.

"And can you imagine what the place is called? . . . You'd never guess! The Emperor's Filling Station. No, it's not a joke, an emperor really did stop here, and I'm sleeping in the bed he slept in. Madame Barbidoux told me the story. Two years ago, the Negus, a Negro emperor, one from Ethiopia, had an accident on this main road, and stopped here with his retinue. After he had enjoyed one of Madame Barbidoux's wonderful omelettes stuffed with olives and truffles, he spent the night here!

"But you know, Zaïmis, I don't only serve gas. I'm learning how to do repairs as well. I know all the greasepoints of French cars now, and foreign ones as well. I use a machine rather like a gun, which goes pchtt! pchtt! . . . It's a lot of fun. And of course I know how to take a tire off and mend it. Monsieur Barbidoux says I'm a tremendous help to him, and he's promised to keep me for good. He's even written to Greece and Holland so that there won't be any trouble with the Home at Lyssira, and I can have permission to stay. Later, when I'm grown up, I'd very much like to drive a heavy truck. It's a wonderful job. You have to be strong and full of courage . . . But I will be."

Here Porphyras stopped writing. He scanned the countryside as if he were seeking something, bent his head, and picked up his fountain pen again.

"Dear Zaïmis, you would probably think that I was entirely happy, since I like my job so much, and laugh and sing while I am working. But Mina has not yet been found.

139

It's five months now since she disappeared. Whenever I talk about her Monsieur and Madame Barbidoux look anxious, and try to make me believe that there is no more hope that she will come back; but I can't believe it. Dear Mina, she would be so happy in this land so like our own. Write to me often, Zaïmis. I shall never forget you, or Piet and Johanna. I've journeyed through many lands, crossed many frontiers, but for all that it's a very small world, and we shall see each other again one day.

Your Porphyras."

He rapidly glanced through the two pages from an exercise book that he had covered with his swift and spidery writing. He was afraid of having left spelling mistakes: he so rarely wrote in Greek these days. He was just sealing the envelope when he heard someone calling in the distance.

"Well, Porphyras, have you so much to say you've forgotten it's dinnertime?"

He walked away from the olive tree that had sheltered him from the sun and came back to the café. The proprietor's table, just by the door leading into the kitchen, was already set.

"I'm sorry," Porphyras said, ashamed of being late.

He sat down facing Toine Barbidoux, who was reading a newspaper. They always had their meal early, so as to be ready for their customers, who came in at intervals well into the afternoon. Porphyras remained downcast. The final paragraph of his letter had brought back too many memories.

Monsieur Barbidoux put his newspaper aside and said: "This afternoon, Porphyras, you'll be the boss. I've got to be away. You'll handle the gas and oil on your own . . . and if anyone wants a lubrication or a tank drained, you could cope with it, couldn't you?"

"Of course, Monsieur Barbidoux, don't you worry . . . and I won't make mistakes over giving change, like I did the other day!"

The prospect of playing boss dispelled his sadness.

"That's my Porphyras!" said Toine Barbidoux. "I knew I could rely on you. You do a man's work already. Anyone can see you're in your element. I believe you like the smell of gas more than any other!"

"As much as the smell of rosemary, Monsieur Barbidoux!"

"It's lucky for me, especially since those new placards on each side of the station are bringing in new customers. It's not every filling station that can offer service in Dutch and Greek! Of course, Greek cars are rare, but from the Netherlands—well, I counted them, and we had twenty-seven in last week, and all thanks to you!"

Porphyras smiled, very proud, and, above all, glad that he was really useful; for it was abundantly clear that Toine Barbidoux was satisfied with his work. Throughout the afternoon he worked without ever slackening his efforts. Now that summer was just beginning, the traffic on the road increased every day. He scurried to and fro between the workshop and the gasoline pumps, while Miette Barbidoux came and went in the kitchen and café. As always, he whistled or sang at the top of his voice while he worked. Sometimes, however, particularly when he was singing a Greek melody like his favorite one, *Beneath the pure skies of Samos*, he would suddenly stop.

"If only Mina were here!" he would say to himself. Then he would rub his forehead with the back of his hand as though to disperse a cloud before his eyes, and start off on a Dutch or French song.

He was in the garage, and was just mending a puncture (which made him think of the nails he had put on the cedar slope), when another car drew up in front of a pump, sounding its horn in swift staccato to show that it was in a hurry. Porphyras was just putting down his tire lever so that he could go and refuel the car when Miette Barbidoux called to him, "Don't bother, I'll go." He went back to his work; but, as he lifted his head to draw breath, for the tire was

141

difficult to remove, he thought he recognized the profile of the driver, who, having paid for the gasoline, was climbing into his car. He started, dropped his tools, and ran out to him.

"Monsieur! Monsieur!"

The driver was revving up his engine to get going again, and heard nothing. Porphyras ran after the car and jumped on the back bumper, gripping the spare wheel as best he could.

"Heavens!" cried Miette Barbidoux. "He'll kill himself!"

The car beneath the plane trees was getting up speed.

"Stop! Stop!" yelled Porphyras.

He might have saved his breath, for the driver could not hear him. But at last he was very much taken aback to see a wild head, disheveled and grimacing, reflected in his driving mirror. The car braked suddenly and stopped with a screeching of tires. Furious, the driver jumped out of the car, intending to give the lunatic hanging on behind a good bawling out.

"Oh, sir!" Porphyras cried out. "Don't you remember me?"

Dropping a threatening arm, the man surveyed the young garage hand in blue overalls from head to foot, and shook his head.

"Don't you remember, sir," the boy went on, "last year in Holland, when you were camping near a farm?"

The man thought back, and suddenly his face cleared.

"Porphyras! . . . You're Porphyras . . . How on earth did you expect me to recognize you? You've grown so much! But what are you doing here, so far away from Holland, and from your own land?"

Porphyras pointed to his blue uniform.

"I'm working at *The Emperor's Filling Station*. I was mending a puncture. I recognized you immediately—I've thought about you so often!"

Then hanging his head almost as if he were ashamed:

"It's partly to find you again that I came to Provence."

142

"To find me again? . . . Now, you had a sister, hadn't you? If I remember rightly, she was called Mina. My daughter went on talking about her for ages; they got along very well together."

Porphyras turned his head away; he found it difficult to hold back his tears. The man drew near, and put a hand affectionately on his shoulder.

"I'm sorry to be so clumsy. I didn't know that . . . that . . ."

The boy raised his head quickly.

"Oh no, she's not dead. She disappeared, but she's not dead—she'll come back!"

To further questions he replied in short, disjointed phrases, sick at heart. They were standing by the roadside, beneath the plane trees, and near the car, the engine of which was still running.

"Porphyras," said the camper from Holland. "I'm terribly sorry I can't take you home with me today. My wife and Anne-Marie would be delighted to see you, but I've far too many things to do. Still, we live fairly near, in Avignon."

"Avignon," repeated Porphyras. "That lovely town surrounded by high white walls?"

"Come over to see us as soon as you can. Tell us all about Mina, and if I can be of any help to you . . . Here's the address. If anything urgent crops up, write to us at once: André Magnol, 17, Rue du Marché-aux-Herbes. Our house is close to the ramparts, and near the river Rhône, too. But look here, you're miles away from your garage. I'm not so pressed for time that I can't take you back."

"Oh no!" Porphyras protested. "My legs are strong!"

Monsieur Magnol shook hands with him, got into his car again, and drove off at full speed. After watching the car till it was out of sight, Porphyras looked at the address on the little white card. As he did so a feeling of despair came over him. He realized that, without being fully aware of it, he had put his last hope in this man. He had let himself believe that somehow Mina had tracked down these French people and would be found in their house.

"No," he said to himself. "I won't go to Avignon. It would be awful to hear them talking about Mina as if she were there with us."

He began to run along the road, eager to get back to the filling station and forget his bitter disappointment.

The days went by, summer had come. Now the plane trees lifted their luxuriant green arch above the highway; the first grasshoppers clashed their strident cymbals in the clear air.

"It's finished and done with," Porphyras thought. "I shall never know now, it's been too long."

One morning, however, he was shaken when he received a letter from Holland. He recognized the stamp with the portrait of the Queen printed on it, the Queen who went about on a bicycle just like her subjects. It was Piet who wrote, telling him about the day-to-day happenings at Kruinen, his own visits to the garage there, the building of a new dike. He did not mention Mina anywhere in his letter. It was as if she had never existed.

"He doesn't want to make me feel unhappy, that's why," said Porphyras to himself. "But he only makes it worse."

Then he flung himself into his work again with all his usual ardor, whistling and singing with all his might, forcing himself to enjoy life.

"You know," said the customers at the filling station to Toine Barbidoux, "your young garage hand is as good as a tonic. It's a pleasure to see his bright face!"

Two days after he had received Piet's letter, Porphyras was cleaning out the garage, conscientiously and meticulously, as he had learned to do it at Kruinen, when the mailman, jumping from his noisy motorcycle, called out to him:

"Morning, Porphyras! Here's another letter from Holland!"

"From Holland?"

He snatched the letter from the mailman. It was certainly stamped with a Dutch stamp, but Piet had not written the address. Porphyras felt the envelope, turned it over, and, as soon as the mailman had gone, went and hid behind an oil drum at the far end of the garage. His hands were shaking; he dared not open the envelope. He saw that it was addressed in Mrs. van Hoolen's handwriting. What had happened back there? His legs gave way beneath him, and he perched on a jack, slitting the envelope with trembling fingers.

"My dear Porphyras,

"Mina is alive! She is well and alive! We have just received the news through the Norwegian Consulate at Amsterdam. We know nothing, except that she is in Norway, and in good health. We were told that they intend sending her back to Holland, since they believe you are still here. But we thought that, now you are properly established, it would be better if she came straight to join you, if that is possible, and we know that is what you would wish. My husband has just sent a wire to the Consulate, explaining the situation. Send us a telegram to let us know that you accept this plan.

"My dear Porphyras, we can guess just how happy this will make you, and you can imagine how delighted we are here, all of us. I'm afraid this is all we can tell you today. We don't know why Mina is in Norway, or why we've had to wait all these long months for news. But she is alive, and she is well. Dear Porphyras, we share your happiness, and we all send you our love.

Maria van Hoolen."

Porphyras read it twice, three times. His eyes filled with tears and he could no longer see the written lines. Mina was alive. Mina would be coming to join him. Could it be anything but a dream? His eyes were glued to the letter; he could not tear them away. Then, even paler than he had been the night he had been found numb with cold at the door of the café, he got up and streaked through the garage like a flash of lightning, knocking over all the oil drums he had just built into a neat pyramid. He pushed open the door of the café, yelling, "Mina's alive!" and burst into the kitchen, where the shock of his whirlwind entrance caused Madame Barbidoux to drop the saucepan she was holding. He shouted again, "She's alive! She's alive!" and collapsed in floods of tears on the tall bread bin.

18

Toine Barbidoux and Porphyras were walking down the Cannebière, that wide and splendid avenue leading to the sea, of which Marseilles is so proud. They had parked the car a little way off, and come on foot to seek out the shipping office. Porphyras was silent, nor did he take any pleasure in the lively scene, the bright colors, the sun, or the salt sea smells.

"You think it's near here, Monsieur Barbidoux?"

After several inquiries, they found the company's office, and recognized it by the Norwegian flag. Porphyras hesitated on the threshold. Suppose the boat had been shipwrecked? Or merely delayed a few hours, or even days, because of storms? That did sometimes happen, or so he believed. He was getting too worked up; he just could not wait any longer.

A clerk behind a counter answered Toine Barbidoux.

"Yes, the *Lofoten* is expected today. Pier number two."

"Any delay?"

"None at all. She should berth at 4 P.M."

147

Porphyras breathed again. Only two hours to go, and then she would be there. For Mina was on board. There could be no doubt about that. According to the telegram they had received, she had left Bergen, the big Norwegian port, five days before. He had read that telegram over and over again, as he had reread the letter, before he could bring himself to believe it. And to make assurance doubly sure, he was carrying it now, all crumpled up in his hand. He wondered whether Mina was changed. He knew she was in good health now; but he also knew that she had been ill, very seriously ill.

Every second or so he looked at his watch, one he had bought with his tips. How he wished he could push the hands along!

"Monsieur Barbidoux, shall we go down to the quay?"

"There's plenty of time, Porphyras. What could we do there? The quay's not at all interesting."

Maybe the quay was not interesting; but the busy main roads were a long way from the port, and what if the *Lofoten* were early?

Yielding to his entreaties, Toine Barbidoux led him toward the sea. Porphyras jumped every time he heard a siren hoot in the distance. He wished he could be whisked away to the top of that white hill, so that he could watch the boat in the distance drawing near. Monsieur Barbidoux and he walked up and down the endless quays to kill time, but if ever they drew too far away from pier number two, Porphyras' steps lagged, and Toine Barbidoux turned back with a smile.

Four o'clock . . . half-past four . . . five o'clock. A boat came through the harbor channel; it was only a small tug. Six o'clock. The church of Notre Dame de la Garde was already gilded by the sun. Porphyras looked up at the sky. There surely couldn't be storms at sea when the sky was so clear?

At last, behind the causeway, a siren hooted in the distance. Pier number two, that until then had been deserted, suddenly came to life. The white tips of two masts could be seen coming slowly forward. There she was! The *Lofoten* had just entered the channel, and was tacking about to come in. She was a long cargo boat with a black hull. A flag waved from the stern, a blue cross on a red ground. Why was she coming in so slowly? People could be seen leaning over the port side. Mina—where was Mina? Porphyras gripped Toine Barbidoux's hand until he nearly crushed it.

"Why isn't she on deck? Why doesn't she come down?"

Toine made no reply; he was as anxious as if he were meeting his own daughter. Passengers and sailors were going up and down the gangplank. Toine went forward and called to one of them, but the man did not understand French and only pointed to another sailor in a gold-braided cap. Toine Barbidoux went up to him and asked whether a girl named Marina Patagos was on board. Porphyras began to tremble. The officer smiled.

"Ah, you're the people who've come to meet her. Come."

They followed him. Was she ill, since she wasn't on deck? The officer halted and pointed.

"There she is."

Porphyras sprang forward. He could hardly recognize his sister. Her hair was long and braided, and she wore a woolen dress with long sleeves, in spite of the warm sun. She had not seen her brother's arrival. As she turned around, a little cry escaped her and she grew pale.

"Porphyras!"

She flung herself into his arms. They hugged each other for a long time, as if to make sure that they really had found each other again. Then Porphyras put his hands on his sister's shoulders and drew back to see her better. Enormous tears were running down her thin, pale cheeks. It was obvious from her looks that she had been very ill. She kept on saying, "Porphyras! You're here! You're here!" and then she said, "How tall you've grown; you're a man now!"

149

During this time, Toine Barbidoux was in the captain's cabin, for the captain had taken charge of the little girl, and looked after her during the crossing. Once the last formalities had been arranged, they all disembarked. After all this time, Mina had almost forgotten the French she had learned at school in Kruinen, and was speaking Norwegian, which is very much more like Dutch. She spoke in Greek to her brother, who asked Monsieur Barbidoux to forgive them for it. The car was parked nearby, but Mina wanted to walk about a little on firm land, so as to get her balance back after the exhaustion of the journey and the rolling of the boat.

"It took so long, Porphyras, I began to believe I should never get here. You've no idea how enormous the sea is! I can't tell you how glad I was just now when we came in sight of this town all shining white! It looked like Greece."

"It nearly *is* Greece, Mina, you'll see!"

Dusk had fallen on the great Mediterranean town, a shining dusk still glowing from the golden sun. They settled themselves in Toine Barbidoux's car, which may not have been very new, but was certainly very comfortable, and quite dazzling everywhere, for on the previous day Porphyras had polished it till it shone. Monsieur Barbidoux sat at the wheel, while the two children snuggled into the back, sitting as close together as they could, in spite of the heat.

"Have we far to go?" asked Mina.

"About an hour by road, and all the way along you'll see olive trees and holm oaks and cypresses."

"Like at home?"

"Like at home, Mina."

She sighed blissfully, tired but happy. Whenever Por-

phyras freed his hand to point something out to her, she seized it again quickly. From time to time they turned to each other and smiled. Hundreds of questions were trembling on Porphyras' lips . . . But not now; he did not want to tire Mina too much. Yet he still knew practically nothing. Everything had happened so quickly. The hospital at Bergen had hurried things up so that the little girl could take advantage of this unique opportunity of getting to Marseilles. He began to talk about the house awaiting his sister, about Monsieur and Madame Barbidoux.

"You'll see, Mina, they're just as nice as Mr. and Mrs. van Hoolen. D'you know, I feel now as though I'd always lived there . . . I wouldn't ever want to go anywhere else."

"Not even to Greece?"

"I don't think so. We've no one there any more, apart from Zaïmis, who still writes to me. . . . While here . . . do you remember those French people who were camping in Holland, by the farm?"

"Of course I do."

"I've found them again. They live quite near. We'll go and see them; Anne-Marie hasn't forgotten you."

"Anne-Marie!" Mina said. "I've often thought about her."

Toine Barbidoux was driving along at a good speed. Night was falling. The cars that passed them had their headlights on. The fields that were golden only a short time before turned to misty mauve, and from misty mauve to blue-gray.

Suddenly the car drew up.

"Where are we?" Mina said anxiously.

"Home, of course!" And Porphyras' tone was joyous. Madame Barbidoux was waiting for the travelers, a little worried because they were so late. She took Mina into her arms and kissed her warmly, with tears in her eyes. The table was all laid, with a beautiful nosegay of flowers in the center. Porphyras himself had chosen the menu, and Mina saw everything she loved most—olives, anchovies, and raw beans. But the little girl was not hungry. She felt as though the floor were pitching under her feet, and that her stomach was shipwrecked. Even so, she could not resist the shining black olives, and Porphyras was beside himself with joy. He kept looking across at Toine Barbidoux and his wife as though to say:

"You see, no one else had any hope . . . but I was right!"

He had moved out so that his sister could have the Negus' room, as it was called. When Mina found herself lying between the cool sheets, she felt a wonderful peace steal over her. She looked at her brother.

"You don't want to tire me, do you, Porphyras? But I know what you're hoping for. You want me to tell you all about it, don't you?"

"Not tonight, Mina, you're too exhausted."

"I feel fine."

"Poor Mina, you've had an awful time, haven't you?"

She sighed.

"Yes, awful. But it's behind me now."

She fell silent, as though she were putting her memories together. Then she began to tell the whole story, sometimes full of grief, sometimes falling silent, or sighing, or even weeping a little.

"Remember that dreary autumn day when I stayed at the farm while you went to Kruinen with Piet?"

"I remember it, Mina, as if it were yesterday. For months on end I was sorry I went off and left you alone that afternoon. I ought to have guessed . . ."

"I was terribly unhappy because of that letter from Greece telling us we must wait till the following summer. I thought we should have to stay forever under that gray sky. And yet I didn't plan to run away, Porphyras. You do believe that?"

"Of course."

"I stayed with Johanna, and helped to make Piet's birthday cake. When she had put the cake in the oven, I went out. It was quite warm, and the sky wasn't as gray as usual. I walked along the road to get some fresh air, and to try to get rid of my sad thoughts. . . . Porphyras, as I was looking toward the sea, I saw mountains."

"Mountains?"

"A long chain of mountains with rosy pink snow on the summit. It looked just like Pindus in winter when the sun reaches only the highest parts."

"There aren't any mountains in Holland, Mina."

"It was only clouds, of course, but I felt so happy. . . . I truly thought they were mountains. So I walked along the dike toward the sea. I went along the beach, on the wet sand. Suddenly I realized night was coming on. The cloud mountains had vanished, but I thought I could see them still. I thought I should find them again, quite near, on the other side of the water. So I went on walking into the night: I didn't know what I was doing any more. Boats were dancing on the black water in a little harbor. I unmoored one, a very small one."

"You did? But you've always been so scared of water."

"I don't know now how I could have done it. But, at that time, I was so longing to see those mountains again, and they were only just out of reach. I jumped into the boat, and the current swept me away. I didn't know where it was taking me. The wind got up and the boat bobbed up and down on the waves."

"Weren't you afraid?"

"Not at first. It was quite pleasant being rocked like that. But soon the wind grew stronger and the waves higher. Water rose up and slapped over me. Then I was terribly afraid. The boat might capsize. I shouted as loud as I could, but the storm drowned my voice. Twice huge waves knocked me over in the boat. The third time I twisted my ankle, and couldn't get up again. I lay in the bottom of the boat, in the water slapping against the planks. I shall never forget the noise of that water! Sometimes, at night, I still hear it! It was awful. I cowered down in the boat and thought I was going to die . . . and I thought of you, how

154

you would look for me everywhere, and how sad you would be."

"Poor little Mina!"

"When morning came, I was frozen. The storm was still raging. There was water everywhere, and nothing but water. I didn't know whether I was dead or still alive. Sometimes I tried to call for help, but there was no more strength in my voice. Hours went by while I shivered in that boat half filled with water. I was terribly thirsty, but I couldn't drink sea water. Oh, Porphyras, I wasn't looking for mountains in the sky any more! And then in the afternoon I thought I saw a big black dot in the distance, and that it was growing larger. The storm had died down a little. I tried to lift myself up to signal to it, but my ankle hurt so much that I fell back. However, the ship had seen me, and came near. It looked like a great black monster. They sent off a long boat to row up to me. Two men took hold of me to lift me out, but at that moment a great wave came and one of them staggered and let me go. I fell back and knocked my head against something pointed—I think it was an anchor. My head felt as though it had been crushed like a nut with a stone. . . . I didn't see or hear anything more."

Mina stopped and caught her brother looking for traces of the wound.

"You can hardly see anything now," she said. "My hair hides the scar. But the point of the anchor made a deep hole. If you touch here, you can feel it."

She took hold of her brother's hand to guide it. Porphyras shuddered; his eyes filled with tears.

"Poor little Mina!"

The child smiled gently as though to say: "Don't worry about it any more, Porphyras; it's all over and done with!"

After a silence, she went on with her story.

"It was only later that I knew what happened after I fell, a long time afterward, when I woke up in a white room in a hospital. I was at Bergen, where the Norwegian ship set me down. Do you know where Bergen is?"

"I looked it up on the map, Mina. It's a long way from Greece."

"They operated on me at once in that hospital. . . . But when I came out of the ether, I couldn't remember anything. It was like rubbing a rag over your slate at school—there was nothing left. I'd even forgotten how to speak French and Dutch, and no one there knew any Greek. Still, one day they did discover an old lady in the town who had lived in Greece when her husband was . . . what's the word—oh yes, consul, that's it, consul in Athens. They asked her to question me. I didn't know my name, nor the name of our village. It was as though a big black curtain prevented me from finding what I was looking for. It was like that for months."

"How unhappy you must have been, Mina!"

"No, I wasn't . . . since I couldn't remember anything. I only began to be unhappy when my memory came back to me, quite suddenly, only a couple of weeks ago. I was in the hospital yard. The old lady, who often came to see me—she was very sweet—had brought me a book of stories she'd sent for specially to Greece. All at once I saw a name in it—your name, Porphyras. In an instant the great black curtain was torn down. I saw Simitra, Lyssira, and Kruinen again. I heard your voice, and the voices of Zaïmis and Piet and Johanna. My heart gave a great leap, my legs began to tremble, I fainted. But I was well again! That same evening I told the old lady everything. The following morning the doctor phoned Holland right away. Oh, Porphyras, I can't tell you how unhappy I was then! I was as ashamed as if it was my own fault that I had lost my memory; I felt afraid of myself, as if I was a monster. Above all, I thought of you. Oh, Porphyras, I felt so dreadful! Luckily that stage didn't last long, for I thought I would die of it. Oh, Porphyras, forgive me! Forgive me!"

156

Mina began to cry. Porphyras kissed her on her forehead, her hair.

"There's nothing to forgive, Mina; you haven't done anything. Just forget all this terrible nightmare. Think only how we're together again, and that nothing can ever separate us now!"

"You thought I was dead, didn't you?"

"Everyone else kept quiet when I talked about you. But I never really lost hope."

She was exhausted when she had finished her adventures. But she still wanted to know what had happened to her brother through those eight long months.

"Now you tell me!"

"Not tonight, Mina, you're too tired . . . and it would take too long. Go off to sleep quickly now. If you do, you'll be ready to enjoy the wonderful Provençal sun much earlier!"

"Ah! The sun! I missed it all the time I was in Norway."

She fell silent. Porphyras held her hand until her eyes closed and her breathing grew slow and regular. Only then did he go off into his own room.

When she awoke next morning, the little girl looked as astonished as her brother had three months before, when he saw the snowy blossoms of an almond tree in flower.

"Grasshoppers!" she cried out, listening hard. "It sounds like grasshoppers!"

"Yes, that's right; it is grasshoppers!"

She turned her head and saw her brother. She hardly recognized him.

"See, Mina—my working clothes, my red uniform of Simitra. . . . Only it's turned blue! D'you think it suits me?"

She smiled at him.

"It's not so showy as the one the dressmaker made at Simitra, but it's much better cut."

"And it's not just for show, either, I can tell you. *The Emperor's Filling Station* is a busy concern. I sell more than

157

two hundred and fifty gallons of gas a day. And as for lubricating, draining tanks, general repairs! If only our poor Papa Christophore could see it! If he could have known that an emperor's car had stopped here!"

"An emperor?"

"He even slept in this very room!"

"An emperor! Tell me about it, Porphyras."

"You shall have the whole story. Do you feel well enough to get up?"

"I was terribly tired yesterday evening, but I'm not ill."

A quarter of an hour later she joined her brother in the kitchen. Madame Barbidoux received her with open arms and was glad to see that she looked rested and in good spirits. She gave her goat's milk and olives for breakfast.

"Everything I love most!" the little girl said, kissing her to show her gratitude. The two children breakfasted together, for though Porphyras had been up for hours, he would not eat without her. Mina had recovered her normal appetite.

"This is much nicer than the dried fish roes I ate in Norway."

Porphyras was dying to show her his domain.

"Do come and see, Mina!"

Outside, the summer sun had invaded every field. Mina stretched out her arms as though she was trying to catch an armful of sunbeams.

"This blue, blue sky! Is it always so wonderful?"

"Always, even in winter."

A long, uninterrupted line of cars flowed by like a river. Now that summer had come, most of the cars were making for the south, traveling toward the sun, so worshiped by dwellers in northern climes.

With his sister looking on, Porphyras refueled two foreign cars, an English one and a Belgian. Laughing, he came over to his sister.

"Did you learn any Norwegian while you were there?"

"A little."

"Good, now we can add it to the placards. I should think we'll be the only filling station in the whole of Provence where so many languages are spoken!"

Then he led her into the garage, and showed her how the car jack worked, and the grease gun. She was full of admiration for his pyramid of oil drums, skilfully arranged the way he had learned from the garage owner at Kruinen. He was conscious of his sister's admiring eyes fixed upon him, and he nearly burst with joy.

"See, Mina, this is what I dreamed of. And it's all come true!"

The little girl smiled—then her face clouded over.

"Monsieur and Madame Barbidoux are awfully nice. But do you think they will keep us both?"

"Don't you worry, Mina. Remember that I'm earning my own living now, and Monsieur Barbidoux is pleased with my work. Everything's arranged as far as you're concerned. To begin with, you'll go to school. You'll learn some French, since you've almost forgotten it. Later, you can help Madame Barbidoux in the kitchen, since you like cooking. But all this is on one condition . . ."

"What?"

"That you are happy here! No more going off in boats!"

"Oh, Porphyras, how mean you are! I know already that we'll find ourselves at home here. When I was on the boat coming here, I was still afraid, because I felt there was only one beautiful country in the world, and that one ours. But now I can understand what you mean, Porphyras. Over there, we've no one. But here you've found work, you're already at home . . . and I shall see Anne-Marie again."

She paused a moment.

"I often think of Holland, and I feel ashamed. What must Piet and Johanna have thought of me? Yet I liked them so much. I would like to see Mr. and Mrs. van Hoolen again some day to ask them to forgive me."

"Maybe one day they'll pass through this place. Sometimes you'd think the whole of Holland was streaming by to enjoy sunbathing by the sea!"

"Oh, I'd be so glad if that happened!"

"And I'd like to see the Bruneaus again—you know, those people who took me in and were so good to me in Paris. Perhaps Monsieur Bruneau will take this road one day with his truck."

Just then a car drove in and drew up in front of the little flower-decked platform where the gasoline pumps stood in a row.

"Five gallons, youngster."

"Regular or Super? Do you want any oil? Allow me to wipe the windshield."

Mina smiled, very proud of this big brother, so self-reliant and so well able to look after her. In spite of all the disasters that had overtaken him, he had kept his trust in life.

160